PROTECT ME

LAUREN BIEL

To the readers who have a little bit of a daddy kink and want to grind on the lap of their grumpy protector, this one's for you

CHAPTER ONE

Vance

I haven't been a legal bodyguard in years. When I got sick of making twelve dollars an hour at the strip club I worked at, I went along with the girls to private parties. Instead of twelve dollars an hour, each girl gave me twenty percent of what she made each night.

And my girls made a lot.

But after a while, even *that* didn't seem like enough. I wanted more. Needed more. And that's how I ended up here, as the personal guard for a member of a prominent mafia family here in NYC.

"Mr. Lore," my boss says as he sits in his leather chair. He puts a cigar to his lips and hands me one of my own.

I take the lighter and light it. The earthy taste hits my tongue, and hazy smoke swirls around me.

"My daughter is getting married in two weeks. Promised to the Vendetti's oldest son. But there's a problem. A few members of their family are not too keen on this union, so that's why I needed the best of the best."

"I wasn't aware your daughter was in a relationship." I usually hear about those things.

He laughs. "She isn't."

I cock my head.

"My daughter knows her role. She's marrying for the betterment of our family business."

I hold back a scoff. I wasn't born with a silver spoon in my mouth like them, but at least I can marry who I want. Well, if I had the time to get married.

"How often does she need my services?" I ask.

"Twenty-four seven."

My jaw drops. I've never done a gig that needs that much of my time and energy. I'm not keen on the idea.

"Boss, I'm thankful for the opportunities you've given me over this last year but—"

"It comes with a two-mill payout," he interrupts.

Two million dollars to babysit his brat for two weeks? Suddenly, the gig doesn't seem so bad. The time and effort don't feel so dreadful.

It feels worth it.

I sit back in my chair. "When does my watch start?"

"I thought that'd change your mind." He smirks. "Tonight, eight p.m. I'll call you with the details, Mr. Lore."

Tonight? I have less than six hours before I'm locked into a twenty-four-hour gig. Fuck me.

I SHOVE my phone into my pocket and drive toward the restaurant. I look in the rearview mirror and stare at my suitcase.

I'm not feeling great about this job. It doesn't feel right. But a two-mill payout is worth ignoring my feelings. I'm good at my job—that's why they hired me—which means they have genuine concerns about their daughter's wellbeing.

And that concerns *me*.

I shut off my busy thoughts and pull into the parking lot. A valet meets me at the entrance. I get out of the car, give the man my key, and adjust the sleeves of my suit before going inside.

When I walk in, a hostess guides me to a room off the main dining area, which looks lackluster in comparison. Golden chandeliers reflect the light above my head, for fuck's sake.

There's a lot I'd like to do with two million dollars, and not one of those things involves golden fucking light fixtures. Waste of money. If they grew up poor like I did, they'd realize how tacky and pretentious these extravagancies are.

The room is empty except for a long family table with fancy wooden chairs running along both sides. It's their own personal dining room, only for those within their family.

My boss stands up and greets me with a handshake. He's dressed much better than I am. His suit is tailored precisely to his body. Maybe mine will be, too, once I finish this job.

"Mr. Lore, I'm glad you came," he says. His hand floats between each of his family members. "This is my brother, Tino, and my wife," he tells me before turning to the young brunette beside him. "And this is my daughter, Isabella."

She stands and puts her hand in mine. I've seen pictures of her, but they don't do her justice. She's fucking beautiful. Big, round, rich brown eyes climb up my body, and her full lips pull into a professional smile.

"Nice to meet you," I say, drawing my attention from her and putting it back on my boss.

I nod to his brother and wife, who don't look terribly excited to be here. They have no reason to trust me, though, not like Angelino does. I've taken a bullet for him, and he hopes I can extend that dedication to his daughter. I hope I don't have to.

Angelino's wife is beautiful and is at least a decade his junior. Isabella looks just like her, except with fewer lines around her eyes and mouth.

"I ordered you the steak. It's our finest cut this evening," he says as he pulls a chair out and offers it to me.

I sit down, and a waiter sets the plate in front of me. A creamy pan sauce garnishes it. My mouth waters at the sight, almost as much as it did at the sight of their daughter.

They wait for me to cut into my food before they begin eating. By cutting into this meat and devouring their expensive meal, I officially accept their order of protection. I pick up the knife and fork and slice into the buttery meat, sending blood-tinged grease across my plate. When I put the tender meat into my mouth, they all begin to eat except for Isabella. Her face draws into a frown and I take in every inch of her expression. This doesn't feel like the exciting union he bragged about. There's a heaviness in the room I can't quite put my finger on, but I'll figure it out.

That's my job, and I'm fucking good at it.

CHAPTER TWO

Isabella

I have a responsibility as the only daughter: get married to the son of another influential family to stack our influence throughout the city. I know what is expected of me, but it doesn't mean I have to like it.

I met my future husband once, and he was a dick. Cocky, self-absorbed, and everything I expected from someone in his family. I met him and disliked him, and then when I found out I had to marry him, I *really* didn't like him. Hated him, even.

But it is what it is. My name comes with a familial obligation that I must fulfill.

A knock on the door shakes me from my wallowing. The person behind the door is likely the man my father hired to babysit me.

I don't want a babysitter. I don't *need* one—I can handle myself, just as I always have—but my future husband's family is fucking evil. Shit, my future husband is evil. But this arrangement is for my family's best interest, not mine, and my family comes first.

I scoff, grab the doorknob, and turn it. The man from dinner stands before me, a large suitcase in his right hand.

"Ms. Isabella," he says as he walks past me.

"You can call me Bella. Vance, is it?" I close and lock the door behind him. "Forty-three, unmarried, upstate native?"

He sets down his bag. "You do your research."

"I don't want to sleep under the same roof as someone I don't know," I say, my voice flat.

"Wise. Where am I sleeping?" he asks.

I gesture down the long hallway. "There's a guest bedroom beside my room. First door on the right."

Vance grips his bag again and takes apprehensive steps down the hall. The outline of his pistol lies against his hip. It's black, like the fitted shirt hugging his muscles.

His eyes dart as he walks past every open doorway, as if memorizing my floor plan. My dad said he was the best. He sure looks the part.

I smooth my skirt before grabbing my coat off the rack. My pockets feel too light, and I realize my keys are in the kitchen. My heels clack against the marble floors as I traverse the maze of hallways. When I reach the kitchen, I grip the keyring that holds my BMW fob, my house key, my parents' key, and a few keys that go to things I can't recall. I slip them into my pocket.

The moment I grip the doorknob, the sound of someone clearing their throat comes from behind me. I raise my eyebrow and turn around.

"Where do you think you're going?" Vance asks.

"Excuse me?"

"I'm supposed to watch you, remember? That means at home, little miss."

I laugh. "I'm not a child, Mr. Lore. You're my guard, not

my boss. If you want to stay home, go nuts, but I'm going out. Unless you want to piss off my father, I suggest you come along, though."

I rip open the door, let it slam, and take a few steps down the hall. The door whips open behind me, and I smirk. I look back and see Vance putting on his jacket as he follows me, the fabric concealing the pistol on his hip.

"Wait up, Bella," he calls.

OUR FAMILY OWNS THIS CLUB, so I'm not terribly worried about much more than getting a strong drink and letting myself enjoy the music. The DJ behind the desk is one of my favorites. Her hair is twisted in braids at the top of her head, smashed by her big headphones. She throws me a small wave as I walk in.

I make a beeline for the bar, and Vance remains behind me. He breaks stride and heads to the left, sitting at a table along the wall. I continue to the bar, get my usual vodka cranberry, and meander to the dance floor.

The music pumps in my chest, pushing its life force through my veins. My hips sway to the beat. When I dance, the music lifts me up and the world around me disappears. The lights dull, the people blur, and my worries melt away.

Hands grip my waist, and I turn to see the strong-jawed man who owns them. I smile and let him pull me into his broad chest. It's so fucking attractive.

As I grind against his knee, I look over at Vance, who's risen from his seat. His dark eyes are locked on me—on *us*—and I can feel the tension in his posture from here. It's like a thread between us, pulled tight and ready to snap. His hand moves to his hip, and I know it's resting on his pistol.

The man in front of me regains my full attention as his touch rises upward. He leans in to kiss me, but I turn my head to let his lips land on my neck instead of my mouth.

I can't fuck anyone, but it doesn't mean I can't have a little bit of fun. Just a little. Just enough to smother the fire that's been burning between my legs for years now.

I've promised to keep it lit for my future husband, but sometimes the heat becomes too much, and the only way to get it under control again is to hump the lap of some dude in the back of my car.

There's no way Vance will let me bring anyone back to my car, and I definitely won't get the opportunity to grind on any laps.

A touch on my shoulder makes me leap back.

"Hey, what the fuck?" my dance partner snarls at Vance, who's trying to get between us.

"You two are done dancing. Let's go," Vance tells me, his hardened expression leaving little room for argument.

The man scoffs. "*She* can say when we're done. Who the hell are you, anyway? Her dad?"

"By proxy," Vance says before grabbing my arm and dragging me toward the door.

The man grabs my other arm and pulls me backward, and I find myself in a pretty hot game of tug-of-war.

Vance does *not* share that same sentiment. He stops midstep and spins around, keeping his hand on me while swinging his other fist at the man. The solid punch to the face knocks the man backward.

"*Daddy* says it's time for her to go. Fuck off." Vance shakes out his hand and drags me away.

Something tells me I won't be having fun anytime soon. Not with Vance around.

CHAPTER THREE

Vance

"You have a lot of nerve," Bella hisses from the back seat. "You're being paid to protect me, not cock-block me!"

I smirk at her frustrated tone. Unfortunately for her, protecting her *does* mean blocking the cock.

"Your father said you have to be 'pure' for your marriage. Remember?"

"I wasn't going to sleep with him. There's more to sex than P-in-V action."

I could have let her grind on that dude, but I didn't like watching her tan thighs on either side of his or the way her skirt bunched up as she danced on him. The movements of her hips caused her lips to part a bit, and her eyes had closed as she put a hand through her dark hair.

Besides that, there was too much distance for me to cross if something went south. From a service perspective, she needed to be closer to me if I had to protect her.

"I'm sorry for clam-jamming you, Bella, but I'm not taking any risks." I'm not willing to, even if she is.

She crosses her arms over her chest. "It's Isabella to you."

Guess we're back to formalities.

She pouts and sits back in her seat. I pull my eyes from the rearview mirror and force them back on the road. Isabella is much younger than me, and she's clearly acting like it. My guess is she's never had anyone tell her no before.

Such a daddy's girl.

But I'm not her father, and I won't be manipulated by her antics. She can think I'm as boring as she wants because I'm going to be boring as fuck for the next two weeks.

I'm not some square, despite what she thinks. I can have fun, and I don't care if other people have fun, but I take my job very seriously.

And right now, she's my job.

Her father would have my head if something happened to his little girl, so I have no choice but to be stern with her. It's what I'm being paid to do. It's what I'm being paid *a lot* to do, so she can throw as many tantrums as she wants.

We pull into the large garage after a drive accompanied by silent brooding. Cars that I've never been able to afford loom on either side of me. Lambos, Mercedes, Bentleys. Maybe I can afford one once I get paid from this gig. I'll get something that has a convertible top so I can feel the breeze in my hair.

I nearly laugh. I'd never be caught dead in a convertible. I like inconspicuous cars, and none of these are inconspicuous. People seek out people in these vehicles. No one thinks twice about a man in a Toyota Camry, that's for sure.

I pull the BMW into its spot and get out to open the door for her. Before I can touch the handle, she opens the door into me with passive-aggressive force. The metal juts into my gut. I catch it, but not before it scrapes my skin and causes pain I wasn't in the mood for.

"Oops, sorry," she says, completely unapologetic. She pushes past me as she climbs out of the car and takes off on long legs.

I exhale and slam the door. "You're being childish," I say as I follow her into her wing of the home.

She spins on her heels and raises her chest. She's speechless, though I know she's overflowing with words she'd like to say to me.

"We need ground rules," she finally says as she steps into me and puts her pointer finger against my chest.

The moment the pad of her finger jabs my sternum, I grip her wrist and twist her arm behind her back, which spins her around and immobilizes her. She squeals, not from pain but from anger.

"I agree," I snarl.

One of those ground rules is going to involve her not laying her hand on something much bigger and stronger than her.

If I didn't need money, I wouldn't even be doing this job. I wouldn't have to babysit such a mouthy, opinionated brat.

She whimpers within my hold and flails against me. Her cheeks puff with anger. She reminds me of a child fighting against the grasp of a parent who's trying to keep them from touching a hot stove or running into traffic. Instead of trying to save her life, I'm trying to preserve her innocence.

Well, in a way, that *is* saving her life. Her father claims to love her infinitely, but even he will find little use for her if she were impure. Love would have to be enough to keep her alive, and I'm not sure my boss is capable of loving anyone but himself and money.

"Don't touch me, little miss, because I *will* hurt you. And watch your pretty little mouth, too."

The heat of her body presses against me and takes my mind to a very unprofessional place. I release her before I get hard. With flushed cheeks, she turns back to me and rubs her wrist. "You can't put your hands on me." She paws around her body for her phone. "I'm calling my father."

I whip out my cell and hand it to her, and she holds the black device in her hand like it's a bomb. She's bluffing. I know she is, and I hardly know her at all. It's just that obvious.

Her cheeks blow out as she forces the phone back into my hand. Her lips tighten into a thin line, and she turns around.

I clear my throat, and she stops midstep. "I was given permission to do *anything* to keep you safe. That includes putting my hands on you."

"Fuck you, Vance," she snarls. "My father wouldn't have agreed to that."

"He did. Guess he knew you'd be like this. A fucking brat."

She storms off and slams her bedroom door.

As I pass her room on my way to mine, I rap on her door. "I'm not your father, Isabella. I won't let you get your way, so I suggest you find a better attitude before tomorrow."

Why do I get the feeling she won't even look for one?

This is why I like day gigs. I deal with a lot of shitty attitudes, but I get to leave them behind and go home afterward. With this job, I'm stuck with her and her attitude for the next two fucking weeks.

I can't help but wonder if it's worth the payout. We'll see.

CHAPTER FOUR

Isabella

Fuck Vance, and fuck my father for hiring him. Against my father's wishes, I'm an adult. I grew up. I did *every-thing* he asked of me, including remaining a virgin while all my friends partied and lost their V-cards. It got to the point where I was too embarrassed to even admit that I still held on to mine.

My friends all think I got laid by some Harvard college kid. Some elite douchebag I met at a party when I turned eighteen a few years ago. We didn't fuck. His whiskey dick wouldn't have allowed him to have sex with me if he'd tried. But I did come against his bent knee before he passed out.

I kind of love that, actually. Grinding on them through my clothes. The soft friction and the way my silk panties rub against my clit make my eyes roll to the back of my head. If sex feels half as good as that, I'll be in heaven.

Can you even have orgasms in heaven, or is that just a hell kind of thing? Either way, I want all of them.

When I lie back in bed and slip my shorts aside, my mind

wanders to last night. To the club. To the way Vance punched that dude in the face for not getting his hands off me.

That brute force was fucking hot.

A feather in my gut reminds me I don't like Vance or appreciate his control, but the tickle in my pussy still can't help but react to his strength. I liked watching his form in the corner, silent and brooding with his hand on his gun. When I was grinding on the stranger's leg, I was enjoying the view across the room instead of the one right in front of me.

But I'd never admit that out loud.

I slide my fingers along my slit, letting my thoughts propel my movement. A moan leaves my lips, growing with every swipe of my finger. These staccato sounds accompany each rise of my chest and arch of my back.

My toes clench as I draw my knees toward my body. Just at the cusp of my orgasm, there's a loud knock on the door, and I'm chased away from the edge. Fucking A.

I pull my shorts back into place and sit up, letting my curled toes touch the cool hardwood instead. "Come in," I say, trying to mask my frustration.

The door opens, and Vance stands in the doorway. He's tall in general, his head nearly grazing the top of the door-frame, but he's like a giant when I'm sitting.

A smirk creeps across his face, and I put my hand up to my red cheeks. I just got caught with my hand in my cookie jar, and it shows on my face. My body still courses with the pleasure he'd snuffed out, forced back by his knock.

"What were you doing in here?" he asks, his eyebrow rising.

"None of your business."

He cocks his head. "You're my business now, Isabella. *Everything* you do is my business."

I roll my eyes. "You're taking this job a little too seriously."

"I take it seriously because if something happens to *you*, something really bad will happen to *me*. Your father will have me killed. If nothing happens to you, something really *good* happens to me."

"What does that have to do with you coming in here like SWAT?"

He takes a step into my room. "I heard you in here and wanted to make sure you didn't sneak anyone in." He turns to leave. "And SWAT doesn't knock first."

"Fuck you."

He spins on his heel, eyes darkening as he takes two long strides to cross my room. His hands drop to my bed, one on either side of me, and he leans closer until we're face to face. A frustrated growl leaves his lips.

"I'm going to try to put this into words you understand, since your family seems to love ownership." His warm breath rolls over mine. "I own you, and your body, for the next thirteen days. I'll keep anyone and *everyone* from touching you. Including yourself, since you want to be so damn mouthy."

"You can't do that." I choke out a laugh. "It's my body. I can do what I want with it." *Lie.*

"No. You can't do anything with your body without your father's permission."

Is he referring to himself?

The stranger in the club called him my dad, and he's old enough to be my father. Salt-and-pepper strands run through the dark, unruly hair on his head.

He carries himself differently than my father ever would, though. He doesn't behave in a way anyone in our business would. He doesn't carry himself with dignity, grace, or power. He carries himself like a murderer. Like a criminal.

I wouldn't be surprised if he was. Even his wide stance and the way his white t-shirt hugs his muscles makes him look dangerous, menacing. And the stern look he's giving me right now makes me understand exactly why my father hired him. He's a predator, trained to be deadly.

But I'm not afraid of him.

I scoff. "Yes, *daddy*," I mock, throwing him a two-finger salute.

"Good girl," he whispers.

He offers a smirk that sends a flush through my chest. Then he pats my head.

Fucking. Pats. My. Head.

That smirk becomes an afterthought, and I just about want to rip his nuts off and shove them into his stupid, condescending mouth.

Thirteen days. Only thirteen more days. And then the real fun begins. My shitty arranged marriage to Antonio Vendetti.

CHAPTER FIVE

Vance

Isabella loves to stir up trouble, that much is clear. She's sitting with some young bag of muscles who's eyeing her from across the table with a hunger that looks pathetic from where I sit.

She leans over, accentuating her chest beneath the low-cut black dress, and reaches for her glass of red wine. He says something and she laughs, and it sounds fucking fake. Not that he seems like he'd be able to tell. This is probably entirely normal behavior around him. Fucking rich people.

She knows I'm watching. I can tell by the way she flips her dark hair, big curls draping down her back, or the way she crosses and uncrosses her legs. All of it has a hidden meaning. And even that has hidden meanings, because it's not like she likes me.

Quite the contrary.

Her fingers curl and drag up her thigh, spreading the long slit in her dress and exposing her tan thigh for my viewing.

Not for the bag of shit in front of her, but for me. I have to talk down my dick because the twinge of excitement I feel is completely inappropriate.

I do not fuck clients. I never have, even when they threw their naked bodies onto my lap. Hard no.

There's not some kind of ethics board for bodyguards, but if I get blacklisted by people like my boss, I'll never work again. Not above the dark asshole of a strip club, at least, and that's a problem. I like consistent income more than I like pussy.

When the job is finished, it's a different story. I *have* fucked women *after* I watched over them. Usually we ended up accidentally running into each other somewhere, and a quick fuck was an A-OK bonus for me.

"Vance? Is that you?" says a voice behind me.

I close my eyes and silently curse the irony. I turn my head and see one of my past clients. Someone I worked for before my current boss, but after the strip club. A weird middle place where I was doing small gigs for men I would never meet in person. I like the intimacy of having one boss who knows just how to ruin my day with a single phone call.

"It *is* you!" she squeals as she shuffles her high heels to the table and sits in the vacant seat across from me. She pushes the plate and silverware aside and puts her elbows on the placemat.

"Hi, Theodora," I say with a pleasant smile. I guess Isabella and her meat bag aren't the only fake ones.

"What are you doing here? This place seems too—"

"Classy?"

She opens and closes her mouth.

She meant that but doesn't want to admit she meant that.

A place like this *is* too classy for me. Rich people don't make good protectors. The poor, the rough and tumble types? Yeah, those guys make good bodyguards.

Apparently, a suit can't mask my status. I look like trash to them, no matter how fine the fabric. Which is fine. I'm not interested in rising to their status level or playing by the rules that dominate their world.

Theodora's big eyes motion to the right, toward the bathroom. Interesting how she wants to sleep with someone as *classless* as me.

"I'm working," I tell her.

She glances around the restaurant, trying to pick out my mark. She twists fake blonde hair between her fingers, and her eyes come to rest on me. "Take a break?"

Am I tempted? Yeah. Really fucking tempted. Especially as she uncrosses her long legs and gives me a glimpse of her lack of panties.

I look at the watch on my wrist and catch Isabella in my peripheral. A waiter has just delivered their meals. She should be busy for a little while.

I'll give myself ten minutes.

One single break.

Without saying anything, I get up and walk toward the bathrooms tucked away from the main floor. I go into one of the rooms and wait. It'd be classless for her to come in here, but I'll give her one minute.

Sixty. Fifty-nine. Fifty-eight.

She sneaks into the bathroom with me, and I close the door and twist the lock. Before I even get my hand off the metal, she's on me. Her rosy lipstick smears across my lips as she kisses me.

"I've always wanted a way to thank you for all you did for me," she says against my mouth.

"No need to thank me, Theodora. It was just my job." I made sure her husband knew she was serious about the divorce. Really hammered the point into him.

Her hands work open my belt buckle regardless, and her

fingers fly into a frenzy as she unzips my slacks. I look at my watch. Eight minutes.

I lean against the wall as her hands reveal my dick with an aggression that's very clearly stifled. She strokes me with long, dedicated movements, her eyes on my face.

Guilt flushes through my veins, and I push her hand away. "I can't do this. I have to go back to work."

She scoffs and wipes her hand against her dress. "Well, this is embarrassing," she says, wiping the lipstick from around her mouth and stepping away from me.

"It's not you, and you know that," I say. I throw her a wink. "You know how seriously I take my job."

"Yeah, yeah." She twists the lock and barges out of the bathroom.

I tug up my slacks and go to the mirror. Smeared lipstick circles my mouth. I wipe at the rouge marks until my skin is pretty much the same color the lipstick once was. Satisfied enough, I return to the dining area. When I look at the table where Isabella sat, the food sits abandoned.

"Fuck." This is why I don't take fucking breaks.

I walk to their table and snag the waiter, dragging him aside. "Did you see where those two headed off?" I gesture between the two empty chairs.

He tosses his chin toward the exit before hurrying away from me.

Fuck. Fuck. Fuck.

This is the *one* gig that will cost my life if I fail. I hurry out the door and my eyes scan left and right, trying to find my bearings while also not boiling over with panic.

The Italian restaurant is part of a strip of businesses and restaurants. One building runs into the next . . . except for the alleyway on the one side that leads to the parking lot.

I break into a jog when I reach the alley, and my eyes

narrow on the back of her BMW. Fog creeps up the glass. The breath of relief is followed by one of panic, and I rush to her car and whip open her back door. She's grinding on the man's lap. I stop her mid kiss, and her gaze rises to me with a hint of disgusting playfulness.

She did it on purpose.

"What the hell?" the guy says, pushing her off his lap as he covers his erection with his hand. "Who the fuck are you?"

"Her daddy," I say, a cruel smirk crossing my face.

"Your father, Isabella? Really?" he snaps.

I pull him out of the car by his jacket and he flails against my hold.

"You're fucked!" he screams in my face.

"And you aren't. Get lost," I growl.

The moment I release the man, he runs off, heading down the alleyway toward the restaurant. Once I can no longer hear his footsteps, I turn toward Isabella.

"What were you thinking?" I ask as I pull her ass out of the car too.

She lowers the hem of her skirt as she clumsily gets to her feet. "Same thing you were thinking, I guess," she quips, wiping at the lipstick on my chin. "If I can't play, neither can you."

I rip away from her touch. "I'm sorry? Are you in a position to make rules, little girl?"

She scoffs. "Watch me."

I wrap my hand around the back of her neck and draw her into me. My eyes narrow. "Real bratty for someone who needs protecting."

"How would my father take it, you think, if I told him you went off with some woman while you were supposed to be watching me?" She tightens her lips. "Spoiler alert: not well."

She's truly the most difficult person I've ever watched,

and I've watched tweaking strippers, for Christ's sake. It's like she *wants* to be abducted. All she had to do was sit and eat like a normal person for ten fucking minutes. What game is she playing?

CHAPTER SIX

Isabella

I hate him. He's a walking contradiction. He can go to the bathroom and hook up with some woman, but god forbid I grind on some dude's dick in my car.

He sure didn't last very long with his little lady, considering he was cock blocking me a few minutes later. The way Vance walks and talks, I thought I'd at least have a solid fifteen to get my rocks off and kick my date to the curb.

Vance has locked me in my ivory tower because of my little "stunt," as he called it. I sit on the couch, swirl a glass of wine, and watch TV in my living room.

He comes into the room with a beer and sits in the chair next to the couch. His dark eyes move to the television, and I'm given an opportunity to study him without notice. I fucking hate how handsome he is. If he wasn't so insufferable, he's the sort of guy whose leg I would grind on. He's bossy and rude, and no one has ever treated me like he does.

"What do you want, Isabella?" he asks, probably because he's caught me staring.

"I want to know why you took this job. Are you broke? If that's the case, I'll give you one hundred thousand right now to quit," I tell him, straightening my spine.

He takes a sip of beer and follows that with an infuriating laugh. "I don't want your money, little girl. I want your father's. Besides, I'm *his* employee, not yours."

I set down my glass, kick my feet out, and lean forward. "Vance, can I level with you?"

"Level away."

"I have less than two weeks until I'm forced to marry someone I despise. I'll become an object to own instead of a human being. I want this time to be my own, if you get what I'm saying."

Vance sets his beer on his thigh and turns his eyes to mine. "No, I'm not following."

"I want to have fun. Fuck around with someone, even if I can't have sex. Because once I'm married, I lose all control of my body. The rights to it will belong to my husband."

"What if one of these Prince Charmings of yours doesn't want to stop at some teenage grinding? What then? What will stop them from pinning your ass down and taking more? Oh, yeah, that's right. Me." He scoffs and finishes off his beer in one swig.

I cross my arms over my chest. "I'm tougher than I look, you know."

"I'm sure you're very tough," he coos.

I don't appreciate his mockery.

"My father's personal trainer also taught me self defense, so I kinda know what I'm doing," I say.

Vance sighs, puts down his beer, strides toward the couch, and towers over me. He leans closer, sending his warm breath over my chest. He sits beside me and pulls me onto his lap.

"What the hell are you doing?" I ask as I try to squirm away.

"I want you to show me."

My mouth flops open. "Show you what?"

"Show me what you'd do when you're done getting your pretty little rocks off," he commands.

I roll my eyes, drop my knees to either side of his thighs, and lean into him. "Thank you," I whisper.

I've played my part, so he plays his. "Thank you? That's it?"

I raise my eyebrow at his subpar acting. "Yeah, that's it."

Before I can climb off his lap, he grips my wrist and holds me in place. "Oh no, I'm not done with you. You can't tease me like that and just leave."

He throws me onto my back like I'm nothing. I kick and fight him, forgetting everything I learned as he leans his weight into me.

"Stop fighting me, bitch, and let me finish what you started."

I scream, kicking and flailing for what feels like my actual virtue. It feels so real. So scary. My fists make contact with his chest and face, doing nothing to stop him as he spreads my thighs with a rough grasp that makes me flinch.

"You think your father's little personal trainer really taught you how to defend yourself against someone my size who wants what's between your legs?" He pins my arms above my head, and I puff my cheeks. His eyes trail down my body and focus on the black shorts covering me.

"Well . . . I wouldn't fuck around with someone your size to begin with. Get off me! Fuck!" I yell.

He keeps his hold on me as a show of force for a few more seconds before he releases my hands and climbs off me. "See? You're playing a selfish and dangerous game, little girl. And that's why you need me."

He smirks as he picks up the empty beer bottle and goes into the kitchen.

As much as I believe I don't need anyone to protect me, he made his fucking point. Even so, it doesn't derail me from wanting to experience pleasure before the opportunity disappears forever.

He returns to the living room with another beer and plops down on the chair with a satisfied sigh. He's an asshole. He's maddening.

So why the fuck did his show of force make me a wet mess?

I cross my thighs and try to ignore the ache, but I'm almost willing to offer him a hundred grand to let me hump his leg so I can get some relief. I open my mouth but think better of it and close it. Instead, I flex the muscles in my thighs, sending a pleasurable rub of friction through my core with every rep.

My lips part enough to let a soft moan roll over my tongue. His eyes are on the television, oblivious to what I'm doing. Or so I thought. Right before I come, he reaches over with a powerful arm and tugs one of my thighs to part my legs.

"I told you, Isabella, no one aside from me will touch you, including yourself. Your body is *mine* for the next eleven days. Try to remember that."

CHAPTER SEVEN

Vance

Forcing her onto her back got me hard as shit. Our little game had me thinking exactly like the men she teases. I just have a lot more self-control than they do.

I pull out my phone and click on the icon for the security camera app I've installed. She's lying on her side in the bed, playing on her phone.

If she knew there was a camera in her room, she'd freak out, but I told her she couldn't play with herself, and I plan to make sure she follows my rules.

Just because Isabella isn't allowed to touch herself doesn't mean the same rules apply to me, though.

My eyes roll over her curves. I lower my sweatpants and let my cock spring from the fabric, aching for release. I wrap my hand around myself, rubbing in long strokes as I drop my head back and imagine our time on the couch playing out differently. That I didn't peel myself away from her.

Yeah, I have bad thoughts sometimes, where no doesn't

quite mean no. I imagine pulling her shorts aside and taking what she's forced to hang on to. Her virginity.

How good would she feel?

How hard would she fight me?

Of course, I would never steal her innocence. I'm contractually obligated to ensure she doesn't lose it. And I've never forced any woman, because I've never needed to. She tempts my inner beast, but she's a temptation I'm paid to ignore and keep anyone else from being tempted by.

It's really fucking hard when she's so tempting, though.

I stroke my cock to the thought of her beneath me, her mouthy words morphing into moans as I make her feel better than any leg she's ever humped.

"Really?" says a voice that makes my cock twitch. I open my eyes and see Isabella standing in the doorway. I never heard her come in. I whip up my sweatpants and look at the now vacant bed on my phone screen.

"What the fuck?" I drop my hand over my lap.

"So you can rub one out, but I can't?" she asks, leaning against the door frame.

"*I'm* not the one getting married off." I get to my feet and walk across the big ass bedroom to meet her gaze head on.

"What were you thinking about?" she asks, crossing her arms.

You. "None of your business."

She throws her dark hair over her shoulder. "I'm surprised your dick even works, old man." She sure knows how to get on every damn nerve a person has.

"My dick works just fine, thank you." I know she can see my erection just fine, because her eyes are locked on it. "The only dick you need to worry about is your shitty future husband's."

Her lips tighten. Did I hurt her little feelings?

"Show me," she says, her gaze rising to mine.

"Not happening." I step into her and force her toward the hall.

She digs her heels in. "Please?" she begs, pushing out her full lower lip.

Fuck.

I lower my sweatpants again, letting my cock fall from the fabric. Her mouth drops open.

"How many cocks have you seen in person?" I ask, wrapping my hand around my length.

"None." She clears her throat. "Well . . . one now."

"All those boys you've fucked around with, and you've never seen their cocks?"

She shakes her head. "It's always been through clothes. Besides, I don't think any of them had something like *that*." Her dark eyes rove over my hard length, and her thighs clench together.

Fucking. Temptation.

She reeks of it.

And I can't do my job if I keep staring it down.

"You gotta go, Isabella." I return my cock to my sweatpants.

"But—"

"Now!"

She raises her chin at me in a show of defiance. "Yes, daddy," she mocks, throwing me a two-finger salute before leaving me alone in the hallway with a raging fucking erection.

I go back to my bed and grab my phone. Just before I click off the screen, I see her return to her bedroom. She lies down on her bed, and her hand goes right down her pajama pants. Her unoccupied hand gropes her chest.

This girl.

With my phone still in my hand, I head toward her room. I reach her door just as her back arches. There's no sound on my app, but based on her parted lips, she's moaning.

She knows the rules.

I go for the doorknob, but it doesn't twist. It's locked. It takes a quick turn of my pocketknife to unlock the door and head inside. Instead of seeming surprised, she lets her back fall to the mattress.

"I found your camera this morning," she says with a smirk. She lifts her phone, which has a view of my room. "And I put in one of my own."

No wonder she knew when I tried to do the same thing.

What a psychotic thing for *her* to do. While I like watching, following, and intruding on people's private spaces, it's what I'm paid to do. It's my job. That's what makes me a good guard, and it's not my fault that it gives me an excuse to be stalker-y.

"What the hell is wrong with you?" I snarl.

"Probably the same things that are wrong with you. I like to watch too, and I can be just as tactful as you. You aren't God's gift to guards." She sits up and runs her tongue over her fingers, which drives me fucking mad. "If I can't touch myself, I'll do whatever I can to make sure you can't either." A sadistic-as-fuck smile plays across her lips, and honestly, I'm kind of here for it.

"So this is the game we're playing?" I lean against the door frame, the same way she did.

"Yup."

"Show me," I say, raising my eyebrow.

Her lips twist, and I wait for her to throw her lamp at my head. But on the other hand, this girl is boss-level horny. She reminds me of a dog that hasn't been neutered, indiscriminately humping every object in the house. I get the feeling she won't bat an eye about showing me her cunt.

"Fine." She stands and lowers her pajama pants to her

thighs. Once they hit the ground, she kicks them away. Like a sinful fucking goddess, she sits on the edge of the bed and spreads her legs.

I roll my shoulders, trying to get the tension out of them at the sight of her. I shouldn't have joined her game. I can't win. The temptation to cheat is too strong.

Against every argument from every cell in my body, I take a leery step forward. Well, every cell aside from those in my dick. That thing is screaming for me to pounce, so I'm really not listening to any part of myself. I'm just existing in this moment when the most beautiful pussy I've ever seen is spread in front of me.

"How many men have seen your cunt, Isabella?"

"None," she whispers. She raises her chin. "Just my daddy," she says with a bite of her lip, and I know she means me.

It's cute when she mockingly calls me daddy and I do the same back, but she says it with a whole new tone this time, and I don't know if I like it.

I brush back my hair, forcing myself to listen to my mind as I take a step away from her. Her father will kill me if I touch her how I want to, in the ways I've vowed to never do. But she stopped me before I could bust, and I'm not in the right headspace.

I want to touch her. I won't fuck her.

I keep repeating it over and over in my mind until it sounds like a pretty good plan. I move toward her and place my body between her spread thighs. Her eyes slowly roll up to mine. I lift her chin.

"This is a bad idea, Isabella. I shouldn't be the first one to see your spread pussy. It's supposed to be for your husband."

"Despite what it sounds like, there's no rule against nudity," she clarifies. "Just touch." She enunciates every syllable as she stands.

She's so fucking close to me. The temptation drips from

her. I've never had to guard someone's virginity before, and I gotta admit, I'm not doing a great job of it.

Virginity is bullshit, anyway, and remaining a virgin until marriage is an outdated practice reserved for the religious, not these royal fucks. They hold it up like it's something sacred. So out of reach. Even though I don't agree with it, here I am, salivating over the thought of taking her virginity and destroying her for her future husband.

Her hand reaches for mine and draws me toward her. I'm strong enough to stop her—physically, at least—but I don't. I let her bring my hand to the juncture between her legs. I let the gasp leave her mouth as my bare hand touches her forbidden skin.

She grinds into my palm. Fucking A. I'm going to be fired. Killed, probably, but definitely fired.

"If I make you come, how do I know you won't run and tell your father?" I ask, knowing I'm already in way too deep if she decides to tell her father about what's happened so far. He'd probably cut off the hand that dared touch his daughter, then feed it back to me.

"Because I don't want my father to take me out of the fucking will, which will happen if I tell him."

"Coming is really worth the risk of losing your generational wealth?"

Her eyes darken. "Absolutely."

I sit down and guide her onto my lap, pressing her ass against my pelvis. I drape my hand over her thigh and slide it toward her pussy. She drops back her head and moans, and her body tenses as I plant my hand between her legs.

I rub my fingers along her wet slit until her clit swells and spreads her lips for me. She scoops her hips, grinding against my lap as she moves against my palm.

I'm so fucking horny. She'll make me bust in my pants at this rate, and I'm way beyond those years.

Rubbing her clit burns my fingers because I know how wrong it is. I focus on small movements, and a quick, sharp moan leaves her lips with every pass.

"Come for me, Isabella, so you can get off my lap before I do."

She moans, throwing her body against me as her muscles tense the closer she gets. "I can't fucking come like this," she says with a frustrated exhale.

"What, do you need a fucking thigh to hump?" I joke.

She sinks into my lap with a heavy sigh. "Yeah, I think I do."

I sigh. "Turn around," I say, taking my hand from between her legs.

She faces me, straddling one of my thighs and bringing her lips toward mine. Like a string pulling us together, our lips clash.

I inhale her moans as she grinds against my leg, scooping her pelvis with every pass along the fabric. I drop my hands to her ass, using them to guide her motions. Her moans grow hoarse as they amplify and she selfishly chases her orgasm.

She tastes like a mistake, with soft undertones of permanent unemployment. But I don't stop her from grinding her pussy against me and moaning into my mouth until she's coming in the shrillest, most beautiful way I've ever heard.

I lift my hands from her ass and bring them to her face, pulling her mouth away from mine. She looks at me with a satiated expression, and my cock twitches.

"I thought you said you'd never fuck around with someone my size?" I say, a smirk tugging at my lips.

She sighs. "I wouldn't, but I *know* you won't hurt me. You've made it your duty to protect me."

CHAPTER EIGHT

Isabella

I snuck out without Vance noticing. He's one of the best bodyguards out there, but I'm better at sneaking around than he is at guarding. He'll kill me when he finds the car gone and has to search for me.

It concerns me that I struggled to get off with his hand, even with his direct touch on my clit. But I came so hard while grinding the length of his thigh.

I'm sure my future husband won't understand that at all. He'll probably hate me for being unable to come from his monster cock and expressive hands. Puke. Maybe he won't have much of a sex drive and I'll be left alone to hump my gold-woven pillows.

Music thumps as I enter the club. My black dress stops mid-thigh, leaving my long legs exposed above my black heels. I get a drink, chug it, order a second, and bring it along to the dance floor. I squeeze into the crowd of people.

My eyes snap to a man in the corner. He's not Vance, but

he's watching me just as closely. He's Ronaldo, Antonio's brother.

He's as tall, dark, and handsome as his brother, and just as crazy too. I swallow the lump in my throat. He's one of the people Vance is supposed to protect me from.

If I stay within the crowd, I'll be safe. It's the leaving that will be the challenging part.

I rub my hand down my thigh, longing for my pistol, but this dress was too tight to conceal it. I hope that's not a fatal mistake.

Ronaldo is vehemently against this marriage *and* my family. Their father is blind to our rivalry because of the prospect of more money. My father is blinded too. Antonio's father told Ronaldo to stand down, to leave me alone, but *my* father didn't think he'd take a seat.

And it doesn't appear he has.

Sweat gathers around my hairline. My plan to dance with a stranger evaporates into the stuffy club air. Even then, I start dancing, trying to fake the confidence I need to get out of here alive.

I feel naked because I left my phone at home so that Vance couldn't track me. Now I wish I'd let him. I long for his presence when faced with a man who wants to destroy me to keep his family's bloodline pure and their wealth intact.

When I look up again, I meet Ronaldo's dark eyes across the dance floor. They bore into mine. He steps forward, melding with the crowd until I only see the top of his head moving through the waves of people and flashing lights.

For every step he takes forward, I take a step back, but I'm not quick enough. Bodies behind me slow each movement, and I keep looking back toward the door. Going outside would be suicide, though.

My heart thunders in my chest as I knock into a dense group of people, spilling someone's drink on myself. A flurry of curse words spews from faceless people behind me. I can only see what's directly in front of me because fear has blinded me to all else.

I take another step back, and my spine meets with an immovable force. My heart sinks into my gut.

"Daddy's here," says a familiar voice.

My heart crawls back into my chest as I turn and see Vance. I've never been so excited to see his stupid face.

"Ronaldo is here," I say, gesturing with my eyes.

"I should leave you with him since you think you can protect yourself," he says.

I cock my hip because I know damn well he won't let anything happen to me.

I turn in time to see Ronaldo emerge from the crowd, his hard eyes on me. They widen when he sees Vance behind me. *Everyone* knows who Vance is. His reputation and skills precede him.

Vance brings his hand to his side, easing his jacket away to give Ronaldo a glimpse of the pistol. He looks big and terrifying, and I'm fucking turned on by it. Why does this drama seem to go right to my pussy? It makes my clit throb, and I switch the weight on my feet, my thighs rubbing together and sending a pleasurable warmth between my legs.

"Hey, Ronaldo!" I call out, sending him a cocky wave that can only come from having someone like Vance behind me.

Ronaldo's lip curls.

"Must you poke bears?" Vance snarls, tugging me into him.

I turn and offer him a flirty smile that comes from the heat between my thighs. "Yes."

He's my favorite bear to poke, after all.

"Let's go," he commands.

He wraps his hand around my arm and drags me toward the door, his eyes jumping between Ronaldo and me as he guides me through the crowd. His other hand remains on his pistol until the door closes behind us, and even then, it hovers close.

Just as we reach my car door, heavy footsteps come from behind us. Vance instinctively gets between me and Ronaldo and draws his pistol, keeping it at his side.

"Calm down, security guard," Ronaldo says, his hands rising defensively.

Vance growls and clenches his pistol grip. Calling Vance a security guard is laughable. I know it's meant to offend him, but come on. He knows he's so much more than that. He has to.

"Get going, Ronaldo," Vance says, his chest rising.

"This is a family matter." He turns to me. "We need to talk, Isabella."

"Talk to her father," Vance says. "That's how you people seem to work."

Ronaldo takes a step toward Vance. "Our fathers are in denial if they think this will work. I won't let Angotti blood taint ours. You dogs don't even deserve a scrap of our wealth."

I put my hands against the car to keep them from trembling. No matter how good Vance is, can he really fight a family as powerful as the Vendettis?

Vance takes a heavy step toward Ronaldo and lines up the pistol's barrel with Ronaldo's head. "I don't give a fuck about your family feuds. My job is to protect her, and I will do *anything* to keep her safe, so if you could just fuck right off, that would be great."

Ronaldo swallows. He surely has a gun, but he could never draw before Vance pulls the trigger. "This isn't over, Isabella, and your babysitter won't always be there."

Their eyes stay on each other until Ronaldo finally drops his gaze and takes off across the busy parking lot.

"See you around," he calls over his shoulder.

"Thank fuck." I sigh as I lean back against the car.

Vance turns around, his glare hard and angry. Deservedly. "You could have gotten yourself killed tonight, Isabella, and yet I get the terrible feeling you still haven't learned and you'll still scurry off the moment you get a chance."

"I—"

"No, don't. *You* are impeding my ability to do my job. I will not lose my fucking head because of you. I won't get killed because an immature brat had to go out and get drunk and dance and find some fucking leg to stick between hers."

My cheeks flush. But worse, his heat-filled words warm the space between my legs. My panties are soaked. I already know that. My eyes round with a fueled desire as he holsters his pistol.

"Get in the car," he snaps.

I sit in the passenger seat and cross my legs, enjoying the friction. "How'd you find me?" I ask.

"There are only three places I thought you'd run off to. Luckily, I checked this one first, or you'd probably be stuffed in Ronaldo's trunk by now and the wedding would be off."

Yeah, he's probably right. And I hate that.

I also hate how thankful I am and how much I want to show him my appreciation with my hand. Or my mouth.

CHAPTER NINE

Vance

We drive in static silence, which is probably for the best. I'm beyond angry. When you're a bodyguard, you tend to avoid trouble, not actively seek it out. Sometimes trouble finds you regardless, but there shouldn't be a big neon Kidnap Me sign pointing to the person you're protecting, which is precisely what she put above her head with her stunt.

She's squeezing her thighs. I see it out of the corner of my eye. Those strong leg muscles flex every time she tenses. I put my hand between her thighs and rip her legs apart.

"Don't you close those legs. You aren't going to get enjoyment after what happened tonight."

Her wild eyes leap to mine, as if the heat from my hand sends electricity through her. They flash with something crazed, feral.

It's fucking hot.

But it can't be.

"Don't look at me like that," I say. "What you did tonight

was so incredibly stupid, and I'm sure I'll hear about it from your father. What will he think of me when he finds out I let you run off by yourself and you came face to face with one of the Vendetti brothers? Do you think he'll let me keep my job?"

Her eyes narrow. "No."

"Then why do it? You want someone else to be your guard? Some uptight prick? Someone who will probably hold that virginity of yours much higher than I do? You'd have no fun at all, little girl."

"First off, you *are* an uptight prick. Second, *you're* also the reason I'm not having much fun." She folds her arms across her chest, and the pouty pose accentuates her cleavage.

I scoff. "You know I don't give a flying fuck about your virginity. I'll put my hand between your legs and please you without losing a wink of sleep over it. I'd let you rub your pretty cunt against my leg if it made you feel good, so long as it means I can stay in the goddamn house."

She sucks in a breath beside me, which humbles me and reminds me of my rule.

"Which won't be happening, Isabella."

"Fine, *daddy*, I'm sorry," she quips, an annoyed fire smoldering in her dark eyes.

I wish she'd stop calling me daddy. I don't like it. It's weird. And she always says it with an attitude that makes me want to bend her over my lap until she regrets every snarky syllable.

My mind wanders to that thought as I drive, and I clutch the steering wheel. I imagine bending her over my lap, the hem of that short dress rising, exposing the full cuffs of her ass. The sound of my hand smacking her ass rings out in my head, going straight to my dick. Her smart-ass mouth would part and let out a whimper.

I shake my head, trying to push those thoughts away.

They're becoming more and more intrusive. And it's feeling less and less wrong.

Isabella sees my erection. She's like a truffle-sniffing pig when it comes to dicks. She reaches out, putting that hot hand on my jeans, right over my cock. I let her stroke my length only once before I gather the strength to grab her wrist and tug it away.

"Don't. You wouldn't know what to do with a cock like mine," I snap.

She wouldn't. If she gets all her pleasure from rubbing herself, I would rip her in half, and she'd probably be a bitch about it. I also can't risk her telling her father anything. What's happened already is bad enough to put a mark on me.

She might be worth it, but the risk isn't worth the reward when she's getting handed off to her new husband soon.

"You don't know what I can do, dickhead," she says, ripping her hand away from my grasp.

"I know what you aren't *allowed* to do, and I won't lie. I might not be able to keep my hands and mouth off you if you keep doing the things you do to me. But you *won't* get my cock. I'll hand you off as pure as promised. Well, almost as pure."

She swallows loud enough for me to hear. Like I just fucked her ears with my words.

I'm not doing it on purpose. It's just the truth. She's driving me nuts and forcing me to shed my dignity and the strength to abide by my own rules. The brattier she acts, the more I want to shut her up with my mouth.

Before I can even stop her, she leans over and hits the button that makes my seat recline. Distance gathers between me and the wheel until I'm barely holding the damn thing.

She climbs onto my lap, and I try to push her away, but it makes me swerve. She leans in and kisses me. I barely keep my eyes on the road over the tilt of her head as her tongue slips into my mouth. I kiss her back. Because why the fuck not?

"I'm so frustrated," she whimpers against my mouth.

I sigh. "Come on my lap, then."

I let my hand drop from the wheel and grip her full ass as the heat of her wet cunt melts through my jeans. She rubs herself against my tented zipper, her hips curving into me in the most sexy fucking way. I imagine myself inside her.

She pants, and soft moans brush against my ear as she drops her head to my neck. I squeeze her ass as she rides the length of my zipper, grinding it between the lips of her pussy. Her body tenses and tightens as her hand burrows into my hair.

"Daddy," she moans, and my cock twitches.

Must she muddle that word for me? It's usually bitchy and annoying when she says it, but when she says it through a moan like that . . . fuck. She can call me anything in that moment and I'd like it.

"Come like a good girl, even though you're never a good girl, are you?"

She shakes her head, and I feel the movement against my shoulder.

"Fuck yourself against my jeans," I groan.

Her movements grow ragged. She's getting close, and the moans become louder and louder in my ear.

"I'm coming!" she screams, her sounds becoming shrill, yet beautiful.

Instead of going faster, she slows her hips, bearing down so that she's riding my zipper harder but slower. Her body shudders and jerks with each tilt of her pelvis as she rides out her orgasm.

"Feel better?" I ask, pulling my eyes away from the road for a moment to brush the sweaty hair from her cheek.

"No, actually," she says, dropping her weight into me. "I

feel like it's not enough. It's usually enough, but now it feels like I need to come again."

I smirk at her. "That's what happens when your body wants more than high-school humping, but you can't have much more." I raise my dark eyes to hers. "Now get off my lap."

CHAPTER TEN

Isabella

I can't sleep. I'm wide-the-fuck awake. Vance is a pain in my ass, so why do I also view him as such a conquest? Something I want to conquer. No. Something I *need* to conquer.

If he were any other man, he'd have taken me by now, especially considering all the times I've thrown myself at him.

He's more dedicated to preserving my purity than I am, and I'm the one it belongs to. Well, it's a part of me, but it doesn't *belong* to me. It belongs to *him*. My future husband. The man who will set me on a path to become a bitter woman like my mother.

If my father knew how unhappy my mother was, maybe he wouldn't try to arrange my marriage like his father did for him. Marrying for prosperity clearly works so well. But at what expense?

My free will?

My happiness?

Fuck, Antonio is likely elated to have me as his wife. He

can take out his harbored anger toward my family on my body. I'll get punished for things I had fuck all to do with.

I toss and turn and stare at the faint light on the camera Vance has aimed at my bed. No, I won't play with his mind, because doing so plays with mine as well. And I'm too fucking depressed. The more I think about what I had in my life versus what I will have, the worse I feel.

I climb out of bed and walk to the door. I can't help but wonder if he's already aware of my movements as I step into the hallway and head toward his room. When I get to his door, I half expect to open it and find him inside, awake and furiously wondering why I'm out of bed.

But when I sneak into his room, he's asleep. His shoulders are bare above the blanket, and he's turned away from me.

I make my way across the room and lift the blanket so I can slide into bed behind him. I've never slept with anyone who wasn't a girl or my parents, but as I scooch in behind him, his body heat calls to me. It's something I didn't realize I needed until I felt the warm draw.

For being a fucking bodyguard, he's stone asleep as I nestle up to him. I could be a murderer for all he knows.

"Why, Isabella?" his deep voice asks.

"Why what?"

He scoffs. "Why are you in my bed?" Despite the question, he doesn't turn to face me.

"When I used to have trouble sleeping, I always climbed into my father's bed."

"Daddy's bed, eh?" He finally turns onto his back.

I smirk. "Maybe."

He doesn't move at first, just keeps his eyes locked on the ceiling. "Why can't you sleep?"

"My impending marriage."

"Is it really so bad to have more money than you know

what to do with? To marry into generations of wealth and power?"

Heat teases the backs of my eyes. He's making me sound like a whiny brat. "You have no idea what it's like to be a wife to someone like Antonio. My mother was put into the same situation, and she lost herself to that subservient role. You have to mourn who you once were as you become who you have to be."

Frustration and anger lace each word.

He probably expects me to leave, but when I don't—because I'm a glutton for him—he slips his arm beneath me and pulls me against his broad chest.

"You're right. I don't know what it's like to lose myself to an unhappy marriage, but I know what it's like to lose sight of myself in the big world families like yours have built."

My warm breath washes over his chest and pebbles his skin. His muscles tense and loosen beneath my head.

"What do you need me to do, Isabella?"

"Kill my future husband, I guess." I scoff, only half joking.

His gaze drops from the ceiling and falls on me. His eyes harden and darken. "I don't do those things anymore, little girl."

Anymore? Was there a time in his life when he casually killed people?

I swallow.

The more the thought runs through my mind, the more plausible it seems. The more plausible it becomes, the less disgust I feel. It's kind of fucking hot.

But Vance Lore is *not* going to kill anyone for me or anyone in my family, because he hates people like us. Aside from professional ventures, he avoids our kind at all costs.

"Of course not. I wasn't really asking you to kill him," I say before his hand brushes down my side.

"Why are you in my bed, Bella?" he asks again, his breath

teasing the back of my neck. "You aren't the type who needs comforting. If you sat up and thought about your miserable marriage, you'd just catch your bed on fire with your anger, not tuck tail to come into my bed."

My hand clenches around a loose corner of his shirt. He's not wholly wrong, but instead of catching my bed on fire, my anger about my impending marriage made me want him. Not his comfort. Just him.

"I don't want your comfort." I rip away from him and sit up. The moment I try to rise to my feet, his hand reaches for my shoulder and tugs me back.

"Don't be a brat," he whispers. "Comfort doesn't always mean something bad. I don't think you're sad or scared. I think you want to be touched."

"I sure the fuck do not." I try to pull away from his stoney grasp.

He lifts his hand and shrugs. "Oh, I must have read this wrong. Sorry."

He goes to turn over, and the way he flips shit around on me enrages me. I'm used to having everything on my terms.

Which is why I'll be a terrible fucking wife.

"Wait." The word squeezes out of a throat that does *not* want to beg for attention. But I can't stop myself.

He ignores me and draws a deep breath.

I scoff and lean over, draping my arm across his waist and lowering my hand toward his cock. The moment I graze the hard, swollen head through his boxers, he rips my hand away. I pull free from his grasp and get out of his bed with a huff.

I've come to the damning conclusion that if I was dying and the only thing that could cure me was his dick, he'd let me fucking rot.

CHAPTER ELEVEN

Vance

I like this game—probably because Isabella doesn't—but soon she'll be married off to some prick. My job will be done, and we can all move the fuck on from this.

I turn onto my back. I ache for her, but I can't keep doing this. I'm not allowed to want something so virginal when she's already hanging on to her innocence by a thread. If I had let her, she'd have jerked me off and I would have come in her forbidden hand.

But I stopped her.

Because . . . well, fuck, I don't know why. I guess it doesn't take away from her virginity if I spill my load on her pure skin or put my mouth on her pretty little cunt.

The frustration behind that evil thought eats away at my dignity.

I get out of bed and slip out the door. The carpet cushions each step as I make my way to her room. I push open the door and see her form beneath the weighted blanket.

She's not sleeping. I know she's been lying awake and

thinking about me too. I bet if I walk over to her and spread her thighs, she'll be soaked for me. I wouldn't be surprised if she's a creamy mess from getting herself off. I should have watched the camera.

Fuck it.

I make my way across her bedroom, lift the corner of the blanket, and crawl into bed with her. My cock is already hard from the thought of how wet she might be, and it rests against her lower back as I lay behind her. Before she can say something to annoy me, I hook my hand around her hip and lower it down the front of her shorts.

Her slit is soaked with slick wetness. Her lips part and I expect some sarcastic comment to leave them, but only a soft whimper slips through as my fingers glide through her excitement.

"Is this all from me, little girl?" I ask, my voice low and gravelly.

She shakes her head. "From me, too," she whimpers.

Her words fire me up. I crawl over her and pin her on her back. "I thought I told you that you can't touch yourself."

She scoffs and strains against my immovable grasp. "Well, I did."

"What were you thinking about?" I ask, pressing my hips into hers.

"None of your business."

"You're my business. Including what's in your head."

She blinks. "I thought about riding your lap." She squirms beneath me. "Now get the fuck off me."

What is up with this girl and humping shit like a horny dog?

"I have a better idea." I sit up and pull her shorts aside. Her cunt looks good enough to eat, and that's what I fully intend to do. "Have you ever had a mouth on you?" I ask.

She shakes her head.

I scoot down and crawl between her legs. I breathe in her scent, her intoxicating aroma so thick with arousal. I blow air on her swollen clit, and her hips jerk forward.

"What do you want?" I ask.

"Your mouth," she whispers. "Please."

The way she said "please" drives me wild and blinds me with desire. Isabella never begs for anything.

I lower my face to her pussy, spreading her lips with my tongue. The heat from my mouth sends a jolt of electricity through her entire body, and she jerks as if she's come into contact with a live wire. A surprised moan leaves her lips.

I lick her with my tongue in long, broad strokes between quick and relentless flicks. Her moans lengthen and grow louder as she buries her hand in my hair and pulls me deeper. I take in every drop of sweetness, cleaning her before I cause more to drip from her.

"Daddy," she moans, and not in a sarcastic way.

I feel weird about it, but the word is so filled with her impending orgasm, I can't help but like it.

"Come for daddy," I growl before burying my face between her legs and eating her like she's my last meal before her father executes me.

Her thighs tremble against the sides of my head as she gets closer to her edge, and I shove my fingers inside her tight pussy to see if I can get her there without her needing to hump my leg. A loud moan blows into the air as I sink two of my fingers to her depths. My thumb grazes her clit as I tongue her hood with long strokes.

"I'm going to come," she screams through a heavy moan. Her hips move against my mouth, and she grinds against my face as a warm gush coats my chin.

"Good fucking girl," I growl as I pull away from her twitching pussy and wipe my mouth.

I lie beside her and enjoy the way undying pleasure laces each heaving breath that leaves her chest.

"Wow," she whispers. "That felt so fucking good."

I throb at her surprise. As if she didn't know this is exactly what would happen when I tongue-fucked her. That I'd devour her and swallow every drop of her pleasure.

She rolls over and drapes an arm across my chest. Her hand moves lower until she grasps my dick through my boxers.

I won't stop her this time. I let her warm hand wander beneath the waistband, where she wraps her bare skin around mine. Fuck, she feels good. She lowers the front of my boxers and strokes my length, looking up at me with her big, dark eyes as she rubs the dick of someone she should never be allowed to touch. She swirls around my head until my balls tighten in time with her grasp.

I'm going to come. I'm going to spill my load in her hand.

"Make me come," I growl as I drop my head back.

She squeezes my head as she strokes, and I spill my load onto her skin. It's so bad. I'm so bad.

But she's so fucking good.

CHAPTER TWELVE

Isabella

I wake up nestled beneath Vance's strong arm. Memories of last night fill my head and quicken my pulse. I've never felt anything like that. His warm tongue took me to a place I've never been.

I rub my fingers along my palm, where he spilled his come before I wiped it off on my discarded shirt. I never thought I'd enjoy pleasing a man like that. I loved the way his hips pulsed into my fist and the feral groans that left his lips from my touch.

How could my hand make a man as strong as him so weak? He felt like putty in my grasp, like I could have asked him anything at that moment and he'd have said yes.

I probably could have asked him to fuck me, but I chickened out. I don't know if I can take something as big as him inside me.

My ears perk up at a sound outside the door. I shake Vance's shoulder and he stirs.

"What's the matter?" he asks, wiping the sleep from his eyes.

"I heard something," I whisper.

Vance sits up and slips into protector mode. It's incredible to see someone go from sub zero to a thousand in two breaths. He grabs his pistol off the table beside my bed. I sure as hell didn't notice that last night.

"When did you get your gun?" I ask.

Vance rises to his feet and racks his pistol. "Last night, after you fell asleep. I was too distracted by the thought of your pussy to remember my rule. Never leave your gun behind."

"What if it's—"

Vance dismisses me with a quick wave of his hand. "It doesn't matter who it is. I'll protect you. You know that. Just stay here and let me handle it."

I know he can. Vance is a born protector. A natural possessor. But there's only so much he can do without putting a target on his back. He'd never be safe again if he had to defend me from my fiancé's family.

He creeps forward with calculated steps, and his fingers wrap around the knob before he draws the door toward him and steps into the hall. The sounds have stopped, but I still hear the rapid thud of my heartbeat inside my ears. I get out of bed, dress, and grab my gun from the drawer. He said to stay back, but I've never been one to listen.

"I told you to stay put," he growls when I reach him in the foyer. His eyes dart from me to the front door. When he rips it open, he scans outside with the barrel of his pistol.

Vance comes back inside and heads toward the kitchen, his gun held at the ready as he sweeps the room. Our eyes simultaneously land on a box sitting on the kitchen island. When I step toward it, he shakes his head.

He gets to it first, spreading the box apart and exposing a

single plump strawberry covered in chocolate. There's a note along the side of the box.

For my wife.

He leaves the box on the counter and takes a step back, but his eyes widen as he spots my pistol at my side. "Oh, we're not doing this," he says as he steps into me and runs his hand down my arm to grip my gun. "I'm the only armed one here, little girl."

"I have a right to defend myself!" I'm annoyed with him. No one in my family likes to be told they can't carry. It's ingrained in us.

Vance takes a harsh breath and rips the pistol from my grasp. "You don't need to defend yourself when you have me glued to your side." He pockets my pistol. "Do you know what this little gift means?"

"Yeah. It means my future husband knows my favorite dessert." I step closer to the island, pick up the chocolate-covered strawberry by the dark green stem, and look at Vance.

He opens his mouth to yell at me, but I bite into the delicious fruit before he can.

"No, it means he has a key to your home, Bella." He rips the strawberry's plump base from my hand and deposits it in the trash can. "You don't eat shit from strangers when there are people willing to kill you out there."

"Someone's always willing to kill me," I say, putting my hand on my hip. "I don't live my life in fear."

Vance grips my cheeks with a strong hand. "Learn to. I'm not asking you to be scared of everything, but be wise enough to keep your ass with me and not eat poisoned fruit."

I throw my hands up to my throat and cough, turning the dramatics way up as I pretend to choke.

He releases my face with an annoyed huff. "Stop being a brat."

"No can do," I whisper as I fall to the floor in feigned death.

He pounces on me, pinning my hips with his weight. "Do you not understand the gravity of what just happened? If that was your husband to be, he could have seen us in your bed. Do you know how bad that would be for me? For us?"

I deflate beneath him and sigh. He's right, but I don't think he saw us. He would have killed us then and there, not left a gift. "I know, but—"

"There's no but. What happened last night can never happen again."

I meet his gaze. "You didn't like it?"

He scoffs. "I fucking loved it, and that's the problem."

Despite his words, he leans into me and raises my hands above my head. His lips draw closer to mine, and his tongue slips out to swipe chocolate from my lower lip. I expect him to kiss me, but he doesn't. He draws away from me.

"Whatever *this* is, it has to be over," he says. "From now on, this is a strictly platonic gig between us. And until we get new locks on your door, you won't be out of my sight for a moment."

CHAPTER THIRTEEN

Vance

Everything is a game to Isabella. The lack of self-preservation is unbelievable. Who eats a gift from someone who broke into your house to leave it?

She shouldn't trust any of them when most of that family is so unhappy about the union. I certainly don't, so that's why I wasn't kidding when I said I planned to change the locks.

I don't trust people within their network, so I called my friend. He's away at the moment, but he agreed to come late in the day tomorrow. I guess she'll just be attached to my fucking hip until then. Hopefully, we don't get any more visitors.

We're watching some TV together. No one is talking, which I expected. Isabella didn't like feeling my mouth on her cunt and then being told she won't get it again. She can't seem to understand that it's for her safety. If it weren't for people sniffing around here, I'd bury myself in her pussy every chance I get, but people are coming around when they shouldn't. I have to stay far away from my temptation while simultaneously keeping her as close as ever.

She uncurls her legs from beneath her as she gets up from the couch, and I grab her wrist as she walks by.

"Where are you going?" I ask.

"Bathroom," she says, ripping away from my touch. "And I don't want company."

I let her huff her way down the hall, and then I wait for the bathroom door to close before I get up and follow. I lean my ear against the cool wooden door and listen. It's not that I want to hear her peeing, but I don't believe she's only taking a bathroom break.

Isabella likes to ruffle feathers when she's upset. She likes to get people like me going.

Just as I suspected, a low moan rolls beneath the door. The sound warms my blood and brings me right back to the moment when her thighs clamped against my cheeks.

I shake my head. I'm not playing her game, and that's exactly what it is. A game. Isabella is used to acting up to get what she wants, and what she wants is more of me.

But we *can't*, no matter how much we want to. She'll soon be married off, and I've already taken too much of her innocence and shattered it with my fingers and tongue. I can't risk taking anything more.

Then she moans my fucking name.

The singular syllable rolls off her lips on a pleasure-laced breath, and I want to be the one forcing that sound out of her. She shouldn't be giving it to herself. That was one of my rules.

Against my better judgment, I barge into the unlocked bathroom.

She gasps in feigned surprise, but she knows what she's doing. She's perched on the sink, her shorts on the floor beneath her. Her thighs are spread, and she's not wearing panties. Her fingers move along her swollen clit as she bites into that perfect lower lip.

I step into her, putting my hand on the wrist lying against her mound, and stop her motion as I lean into her.

"Stop it, little girl."

She raises her chin. "I may be your little girl, but I'm an adult."

She sure as fuck is.

And she knows exactly what to say to drive me wild. To make me want to throw everything I said out the window. But instead of giving her anything she wants, I tug her off the counter, turn her around, and push her chest to the granite.

When I turn my body toward her side, I pin the back of her neck with one hand as I slide my free hand down her back. "You might call me daddy, but you sure don't listen to a fucking word I say, do you?"

She shakes her head and relaxes against the countertop. My hand rides along her ass, gliding over the incredible curves that make me weak. I ball her hair at the nape of her neck, and she whimpers as I crane it back.

"I walked in on you rubbing your pretty little cunt, but I remember telling you not to touch yourself. Didn't I?"

"Yes, daddy," she moans.

"Do you know what happens to bratty little girls who disobey?" I rub my hand over her skin before raising it and bringing it down on her ass in a hard slap.

She whimpers and tries to pull away from the pain, but I rub my hand along her skin, comforting it with the warm heat of my palm.

This daddy thing isn't something I'm totally comfortable with, but she seems to have grown to love it. Letting her call me daddy is just one more thing I do for her.

I draw back my hand and give her another harsh spanking. She moans and squeezes her thighs together, but I put my hand between them and pull them apart.

"Keep those pretty little thighs spread for me. I want to see how wet you get from this."

She growls. "Why does it matter? You won't do anything about it."

I spank her again. "I know I won't. But that doesn't mean I don't want to see how dripping wet your cunt gets for me."

Her ass cheeks redden to a beautiful hue, and I smack her again, rubbing the pain away with my palm. Turning her whimper into a moan. By now, her slit is gleaming with wetness. She looks good enough to fucking eat, and I really wish she didn't.

"Please, daddy, can I have another?" she begs.

Yeah, she is testing every ounce of my resistance.

I oblige her, giving her the hardest smack of all, and it pushes her forward. She grips the sink to brace against my strength, and her thighs quiver as if every hit sends vibrations through her entire body.

"I need to come, please," she pants.

I pull my hand from her and tug her up by her hair. Her lips are so close to mine.

"That's not going to happen," I whisper.

She blows out a frustrated breath. I'm frustrated too. I'm aching for her, but we can't.

And if I can't get relief, neither can she.

CHAPTER FOURTEEN

Isabella

I fidget in bed. The darkness hides his features, but I know Vance is asleep in the chair across the room. The gun is probably on his lap. He wasn't kidding when he said he would keep me attached to his hip. I hate being attached to someone I can't touch, even when I beg for it.

I squeeze my legs together, the frustration from earlier still coursing through my body. Vance spanked me so hard that he left bruises where his fingertips dug into my ass.

I sigh and get out of bed, pausing in case Vance stirs when my feet touch the floor. I leave the bedroom in my nightgown and head to the kitchen. When I pour myself a drink, I can only hope it will calm the energy between my legs.

Vodka. My favorite.

I put the glass beneath the freezer's ice maker and fill it halfway. The ice spreads as the clear, expensive liquor smothers it. I take a heavy sip, enjoying the burn at the back of my throat. And then another. With the glass tilted to my lip, I hear my door slam.

Fuck.

Vance shows up in the doorway. His lips are drawn tight. "What did I say about staying by my side until tomorrow?"

"It's a quick trip to the kitchen. Relax."

"I swear to god. You won't learn until you're abducted, will you?"

"Probably not even then, to be honest." I throw back the rest of my drink. "I don't like being treated like a child."

Vance steps into me, his warm breath making goosebumps rise on my chest. I scoop up one of the ice cubes, and the cold bites my fingers. I bring it to my mouth as I stare into his selfish soul. His eyes are on me as I spread my lips and take the cold block into my mouth. A low growl leaves his throat.

"Don't tease me like that, little girl," he whispers, a frustrated exhale moving over his lips. "I've been thinking about your mouth for *way* too long."

"Take it, then," I say as I pop the ice cube out of my mouth.

He shakes his head. "You know I can't."

The ice melts in my hand, sending a line of water dripping from my palm to the floor. My eyes darken as I tip my hand over my chest, letting the water slide between my breasts.

Vance reaches into the glass and pulls out another ice cube. He puts it between his teeth, leans into me, and tears down the straps of my nightgown. The thin fabric falls, exposing my chest.

He growls before dropping his mouth to my breast and using his tongue to move the cold square along my left nipple. It stiffens against the ice. He balances the ice cube on his lips and runs it up one breast and down the other, hovering over my right nipple. I gasp as the soft sensuality conflicts with who he is on every level.

I clench my thighs.

He's playing my game. I know damn well he won't give me anything I want.

Even so, I play into his fleeting touch because I'm overcome by a carnal need that just isn't being met. I don't think it ever will be.

Vance leans me against the counter and drops the ice cube to the floor before he tongues my nipple with the warming heat of his mouth. I moan and drop back my head, burying my hand in his hair. His fingers trail up my bare thighs, and just when I think he's going to touch the spot I want him to touch the most, he stops his ascent. His fingers tease and titillate my upper thighs, right before the juncture between my legs.

"Please," I beg. And I hate myself for it, but I *ache*. I physically ache to feel his touch inside me.

He rises from my chest and brings his mouth so disgustingly close to mine. "I like when you beg, Isabella."

I scoff.

"I bet you'd do anything I asked if it meant you could tend to that ache in your cunt, huh?"

I roll my eyes, but he's right. I would drop to my knees and beg for his mouth to be anywhere besides my tits. I'd ride his face like a madwoman if he'd let me.

He'd never let me, though. Because of his "morals." His "pride." His "dignity." Fuck all of those things. I would give up all that's meant to be holy in my matrimony to come on his face again. Why can't he?

I lean in to kiss him, but he squeezes my cheek and pushes me back.

"We can't do that. As much as I want to."

"Jesus fucking Christ, Vance. Why tease me like that?"

He smirks. "So that you'll know how I've felt since the day I got here. Teased as fuck." He swallows. "Now get your sexy ass back to bed."

I huff. "Yes, daddy," I say with a groan as I pull up the straps of my nightgown.

He plays a fair game, and I don't like it. I will up my game if I have to. I've never taken kindly to not getting my way. I always get what I want, and right now, that's Vance.

CHAPTER FIFTEEN

Vance

My back cracks as I get up from the chair in her room. Each vertebra sings the song of an uncomfortable night's rest. I walk past her. She's still in her bed, her lips softly pouting as she sleeps.

My cock hardens when I recall last night, and I really wish it didn't. I get quite the rise out of getting Isabella going. Her cheeks get so warm and flushed when she's turned on. Even before she starts clenching her thighs in discomfort, the mask on her face showcases her arousal. Just the thought of it drives me insane.

I go to the kitchen and make some coffee. The fuel is needed because I slept like shit. I stare at the small puddle of water left by the melted ice cubes, and my mind goes to how her nipples looked and tasted. How much I wanted to wear her thighs like earmuffs.

My phone buzzes, and I look at the camera alert. She's stirring awake.

I stare at her on the screen as she puts her feet to the

floor and raises her eyes to the camera. I know that look. She's going to fuck with me, and I haven't even had my coffee yet.

Like clockwork, her hand slips between her legs. She leans back, spreading her thighs for the camera. For me.

I abandon my coffee and march back to her room. When the door opens, her jaw drops, and she gasps as if she didn't know I've been watching her.

"What's my rule?" I ask as I step into her and halt her movements with a firm grasp on her wrist. It's a stupid question because we both know the answer.

She raises her eyes to me and bites her lip. She's probably still soaked from when I teased her. She might still be aching for me.

"That I can't touch myself," she says. She knows the rule in and out, and she's tried to find ways around it. "But it's hard to follow that rule when I'm so horny I can't think straight."

I sit next to her and drag her onto my lap. The heat of her pussy warms the front of my pants. When she starts to move her hips, I grip them and hold her in place.

"I know you want to come, but you can't," I say. "Neither can I. I'm aching for you. Can you feel how hard my cock is for you?"

She nods before burying her face in my neck.

"Goddamn it, Bella. I can't be around you without wanting to play with you. The only way to keep me from touching you is to tell your father to hire someone else. I have to leave before I make a career-ending mistake."

"Don't do that," she says as she moves to look up at me. "If you do, he'll *know* something happened between us."

"Then can you make it a little easier for me and stop teasing me with that perfect cunt?" I tug her down by her hips, letting her graze my cock through my pants. Just once.

"I want you to be my first," she says.

I scoff. "That absolutely will not happen. Get that idea out of your head. Your first will be your shitty husband, as your god intended."

"I trust you, though."

I brush back her hair and pull her into me. "Don't trust me. I'm not the lover you need."

"And Antonio will be?"

"He has to be. Now get off my lap, little girl."

She reaches between us, undoes my slacks, and pulls down my boxers as she takes out my cock. I try to stop her, but her warm hand feels so good on me.

She moves closer, lifts herself, and lowers her heat over the bare length of my dick. She scoops her pelvis, rubbing her wet slit against my cock.

I grip her hips and stop her, but she wraps her arms around me and rides my length. Back and forth. Back and forth. Her moans elongate as she grinds on me. Every time her warm, wet slit brushes against the head of my cock, I jerk. I've never wanted to be inside anyone so badly.

"Daddy," she moans.

I'm so fucking weak, so lost in the temptation of wanting to lift her and bring her down on my dick instead of letting her rub against the length. How can anyone be this close to something they want more than anything and not act on it?

But I have to.

"Come for me like a good girl so I can make you taste yourself on me."

She gasps at my words, and I nearly do too. I didn't mean to say that. That shouldn't have come out of my mouth. But it did, and now I'm thinking about stuffing her bratty mouth with my cock.

Isabella's motions grow jagged. She squeezes me, putting her body tight against mine as she gets so close. The pulse of her impending orgasm throbs against my dick. Then she stops moving, and her clit twitches against me. She moans in my ear as she experiences a delicious orgasm I can almost taste on my tongue again.

"Thank you," she pants.

I brush her sweaty hair away from her face without saying anything. I keep making mistakes with her. I'm not the man for this job.

I stand up, helping her to her feet before I take a few steps toward the door while pulling up my pants.

"Wait!" she calls after me.

I turn around, keeping my hands on both flaps of my pants but waiting to zip them up.

Her cheeks flush. "I want to taste myself on you."

Bad idea, self. Do *not* let her put her mouth on you. Her mouth would be a gateway.

Despite arguing internally with myself, my hands drop from the fabric and tug my boxers down again. "Come taste yourself, then," I growl.

She steps closer and I lean back against the closed door. Once she's in front of me, I help her to her knees with a rough grasp on her shoulder.

I'm making a big fucking mistake, but I want that mistake more than anything right now.

As she looks up at me with those big, round eyes, I bring the head of my cock to her lips. She spreads them to take me into her mouth, and I groan the moment her warmth wraps around me.

She's lacking her usual confidence. Her teeth graze my skin, but I let her figure out her teeth and tongue.

"This is the first cock you've ever had in your mouth, huh?" I grab the back of her head and push deeper into her mouth. "How about in your throat?"

She gags, but she settles onto her heels and loosens her throat for me.

"Yes, open your throat, just like that." I wrap her long, dark hair around my hand and thrust my hips against her mouth. "Whose come do you want down your tight throat?" I ask as I pull her off my cock.

Drool clings to her lower lip. She looks like she doesn't know if that's what she wants. If she told me to come somewhere else, I would. Her face. Her perky tits. But she rolls her eyes up to mine.

"Daddy's," she whispers.

Fuck. As much as I find it weird, hearing her beg for her daddy to fill her throat brings me to the edge of insanity.

I put her on my cock again and bring it to the back of her throat. She gags, tears marking her cheeks. I thrust against her mouth until I come too. Hard. Harder than I've ever come. Maybe because she's so forbidden, and nothing feels better than something you aren't supposed to experience.

I pull her from her knees before she can swallow or spit. I have no clue what she wants to do, and I'm not sure if she does, either.

"Spit or swallow?" I ask.

She tosses her head back and swallows. She gags, her throat moving heavily. Her lips spread, and she shows me that she took all of it.

I pull her into me and kiss her, exploring her mouth with my tongue. She tastes like my come. Like my little whore.

Only after my cock is spent does the regret swell inside me. How can something that feels so good be this fucking wrong? For Isabella, orgasms are worth the risk of death. I'm not sure I value pleasure the same way, but *she* makes that fate seem a little less dreary.

CHAPTER SIXTEEN

Isabella

My silk dress drapes my skin. It feels so light and sensual. Once dressed, I go to my desk and sit down in front of the vanity. Mascara elongates my already full lashes. Black eyeliner traces my dark eyes, lifting into wings by the corners of my eyes. Dark waves of hair fall over my shoulder, and I shake out the curls shaped into it. Cherry vanilla perfume is the last step in my routine, and I spritz it around me, filling the air with the familiar scent.

I'm dreading tonight.

But I have no choice.

The Vendettis invited me to dinner, which means it's not an option. It may have come across as an invitation, but it's merely a polite demand.

I throw my jacket over my long red dress and head toward the door, but Vance stops me by gripping my arm as I walk by. He tugs me into his chest, and his warmth engulfs me. I breathe in his masculine scent, saying nothing as his chest rises and falls behind me.

"You think you can go alone? That's cute."

My eyes rise to meet his. "I was told to come alone."

He scoffs. "There's no such thing anymore, Bella. Until this gig is up, you and I are one and the same. If you're invited somewhere, so am I."

My eyes narrow on him. "You're going to get yourself killed. For what? Me?"

I'm baiting. I want him to say I'm worth the risk. But he won't tell me, even if he thinks it.

I should be nervous about going alone, but the brothers won't do anything in the presence of the man who set up this whole sordid mess. They'd never act out of place in front of their father.

I can't say the same thing if I walk in with Vance behind me. His presence could shift the tone of the entire room. But I know he won't let me go by myself, even if it makes things more difficult for both of us.

"Let me get dressed," he says, and when he turns to walk away, I glance at the car keys on the table beside the door. He catches my gaze out of the corner of his eye and swivels around to snatch them away.

"Fine, but hurry up. I'll be late!" I say.

He doesn't respond as he disappears into his room.

I drop onto the chair with a snarl. It's not just how he'll affect everyone that worries me. There's so much more to why I don't want him there.

First, how can I eat dinner with my future husband's family while dirty thoughts of Vance plague my head? I also can't stop thinking about him because I have unwanted feelings for him. Or my pussy has feelings for him. Either way, *something* inside me feels *something* for him.

His bedroom door slams, and he comes down the hall looking like a pre-dinner snack. A crisp black suit hugs his muscles, and I want to say fuck this dinner and climb him like a tree, but I have obligations, and those obligations don't involve Vance.

"Can you pick up your jaw, little girl? It's creepy," he says as he passes me and walks out the door.

I blow out an annoyed breath. My jaw was *not* on the floor. If anything, my metaphorical panties were.

I follow him to the car. My skirt rides up my thighs as I sit down in the low sedan. Vance closes the door behind me before getting into the driver's seat.

"This is a bad idea," I remind him one last time.

"So is this," he says, gesturing between us.

"Playing around with me isn't going to get one or both of us killed!" I screech.

Vance cocks his head at me. "Playing with you could *definitely* get me killed. Maybe even you. Depends on how your father would feel about his soiled daughter after I take every drop of your innocence."

My cheeks flame hot at his words. I've never wanted to be more soiled in my fucking life. I tug down my hem and squeeze my thighs together to control the renewed ache.

Vance starts driving, and my mind goes to riding his lap as he drives. My clit swells. It fucking hurts. I want nothing more than to climb over this console and hump him, but I can't.

It's bad enough that my cheeks will carry the red glow into the Vendetti home. I'm not sure how much of my innocence will seem depleted when they look at me. How much of Vance's touch can they see through my eyes?

"You'll have to get me off before we go in there, Vance," I whine.

His eyebrow rises. "Why?"

"Because I can't focus if I'm this fucking horny. They'll know about us! It's all over my face."

He smirks. "Get it off your face, then." His hand drops to

my thigh. "I'm not getting you off. I want you to be blind with arousal when you go to dinner with your future husband. I want you to think of nothing but me as you sit across from him."

Evil. He's fucking evil.

So why do I want to be ravaged by his darkness?

CHAPTER SEVENTEEN

Vance

Before we even step on the landing, the front door whips open and I come face to face with Isabella's father. His face twists into a tight frown, and his eyes scan behind him.

"Why are you here?" he asks me in a harsh whisper.

"What do you mean? I'm doing my job. The one you hired me to do." I respond with the fakest fucking pleasantry.

"No, I asked you to watch her." He rubs the bridge of his nose. "Not here. You can't be here."

I look behind him. Now I definitely feel the need to be here since he's so dead set on me *not* being here. I don't like how it feels. Who hires someone to guard their daughter, then calls them off the clock before she enters the wolves' den? Does he think he can protect her? His self-interest is clearly greater than his love for his daughter.

"With all due respect, I plan to do my job," I say.

"If you don't leave, you won't get paid."

Oh no, no. I haven't been on this babysitting gig for this long for him to renege on payment. I didn't work for free.

Well, free-ish. I got some fun out of it. Either way, I will go back to my roots if he tries to withhold payment from me. He forgets what makes me such an efficient guard.

"You hired me to keep your sweet little angel in my sight at all times, and what you're asking me to do now doesn't align with that. I don't tell you how to do your job, sir, so don't tell me how to do mine. If you don't want to put me on any more gigs because of my dedication, so be it, but I'm finishing this one right. So please move aside before I take her right back home and shit on your dinner plans." I raise my chest, pretty sure I've already shit on whatever his plans were tonight.

His mask of anger twists further, but just before he speaks, a hand grabs his shoulder and pulls him back a step.

"Isabella and Mr. Lore, I expected you to come along. Quite the guard you got for her, Angelino," Mr. Vendetti says. He reaches a well-groomed hand toward me, with the crispest fold I've ever seen in his expensive suit sleeve. "My son has been awaiting your arrival. Shall we?" He crooks his elbow and offers it to Isabella, and she tucks her arm in his as he leads her away. I follow, giving her father a killing glare as I pass. Fucking rich people. Never an unshady one in the bunch.

Jealousy rakes my spine and nestles in my lower gut at the sight of him leading her into a den of wolves. It's becoming real. Too fucking real. I don't like this one bit, and I'm not sure if it's the overall shadiness or because I kind of hate the thought of her with her future husband and his skeezy dad.

We walk into a giant kitchen that's bigger than my entire home. Waitstaff stand by double doors, awaiting orders. It's so fucking weird. Having staff on standby is a luxury I will never have or get used to. Even with a million dollars, I have so many other things I'd rather do than hire someone to stand outside the bathroom door, waiting to wipe my ass on command. I can perform all the basic necessities on my own, thanks.

Mr. Vendetti pulls out the chair for Isabella, and she takes a seat. One of the waitstaff guides me toward a seat across from her, but I force my way next to her instead. Her shit husband can sit across from us. I want to see his face as he talks. I want to get a read on him. Will he treat my girl right?

I clear my throat as the insanity of that thought reaches my rational mind. She's not my girl. She's not mine at all. And I know that. She's promised to this shitty family, not someone like me.

Antonio comes into the kitchen, followed by the shit brother I've already met. Unfortunately. He recognizes my presence and curls his lip. Her future husband also stumbles over his words at the sight of me.

"I didn't expect your help to come along," he quips, and I'm about a cunt hair away from pulling my gun and shooting him square in the forehead.

"Just doing my job," I say, trying to be a little less homicidal about it. I know these kinds of people, and I shouldn't expect anything different.

"So commendable," his brother says with a sarcastic laugh. I can't help but wonder if Antonio knew his brother tried to kidnap her. That he probably planned to kill her. Would they be so buddy-buddy with each other then? Or does no one in these families have a genuine connection with each other? Seems like everyone will turn on everyone, and I don't know how they live in a world with so little dignity.

"Isabella," Antonio says, pointing at his side like she's a dog.

I see red.

What surprises me and dulls the crimson hue is that Isabella gets right up to walk around the table and greet him. He leans in and kisses her on the mouth, and that fleeting touch makes me just as homicidal as when he called me the help. But when she turns her face to glance at me, her big eyes rounding with flirtation, I realize what she's doing.

She's doing this on purpose.

She's giving in to that man because she knows exactly what it's doing to me.

It's making me fucking rabid, and she loves it. She's playing a risky game in their own house. Their home turf. I'm a *really* good shot, but I'd be grossly outnumbered.

Don't play, little girl, I mouth toward her. I'm not sure she can read my lips, but she better fucking stop.

She smirks, throwing her hip to the side and leaning closer into him. He's clearly loving what he perceives as power, but it's not power. He's being played for a fool.

She doesn't want him.

She wants *me*.

There's not a chance in hell that she'll be a good girl for me this evening. She'll be a *very* bad one. And it could get us killed. Not that she cares about that. But I kinda do.

Kind of.

She sure knows how to make a really awkward dinner more uncomfortable by eye fucking me at the table as she sits so close to her future husband. Every so often her gaze leaves Antonio's and meets mine as she takes a sensual sip of wine. It's not how any girl drinks wine unless she wants you to envision your dick touching those lips. And believe me, I am. My dick hardens at the thought of it, and I move my black fabric napkin to my lap to hide it.

Stop, I mouth, and she throws me a sinister smirk. She's willing to get us killed just so she can get my dick hard beneath this fancy fucking table.

Dinner is served, and the staff puts plate upon plate of food in front of us. I'll admit, this shit looks delicious. One thing rich people can do is serve the best food. They probably have Gordon Ramsey back there, for fuck's sake.

I lift my fork while everyone else waits for Mr. Vendetti. It's probably some respect thing, but I'm starving and I don't have respect for any of these people. I start eating because who the fuck cares? I'm not one of them, even if I'm babysitting one.

Mr. Vendetti walks into the room, commanding the attention of everyone but me. He starts talking about the impending nuptials, and I chew louder in hopes of drowning it out. I don't really want to hear about it. I don't care about the fancy decisions they need to make. A horse and carriage? A champagne fountain? *Millions* of dollars in rich-people bullshit to create a fake fucking wedding where the bride-to-be would probably rather drown herself in that champagne fountain than marry Antonio. Isn't there something better to do with that kind of money?

I scoff, and Isabella kicks me under the table. Why? Scoffing isn't kosher but her single-focus mission to keep me hard at this miserable dinner is a-okay? I can't wait to get back to her swanky mansion, and I never thought I'd say that.

The conversation drags on about the wedding, but the sounds become background noise when I feel Isabella pawing at my lap as she slips her hand beneath the fabric napkin. I grab her wrist, trying to keep a straight look on my face. We are *not* doing this here. She has a death wish, I swear. Her fingertips curl along my hardened length, teasing me.

Fucking A.

I scoot my chair a little closer to the table and loosen my grip on her wrist. She rubs the palm of her hand along my length, putting pressure on my head as she passes it. The subtle touch causes the most intense pleasure. Maybe it's because we're in a room of people I hate, or maybe it's the risk, but every touch is electric and dangerous.

Her fingers move to my zipper and ease it down. She pulls my cock from the slit in my pants and strokes me. The huge, flared wooden table keeps my lap hidden beneath it, but as her hand wraps around me and begins stroking, I'm trying to keep my emotions hidden too. I'm trying to keep my face still and expressionless as she swirls around my head. A moan settles in my throat, wanting to come out and spill across this fancy plate. But a moan would get us caught. I curl my fingers around my fork, digging my nails into my palm. She's going to be in so much trouble for this. If we make it out of here alive.

I'm going to come. Each stroke brings me closer and closer. Somehow she keeps her upper arm so motionless except for the little flex in the muscle. Thank god. But the groan that wants so desperately to leap from me is making me restless. Uneasy. Not sure if I can come without making a single peep, especially when she's pulling so much pleasure from me with her touch. This girl strokes a dick once and becomes a fucking expert.

I draw my hand to my lips, setting my chin on my palm. My lips part as the head of my cock twitches, and I spill my load on her pretty little hand in front of her future husband. I try to hide the soft exhale as I finish coming. Right in front of their faces, she cleans my pleasure from her skin with disturbing confidence. She draws her hand away, wiping it off with her napkin as if she was simply removing a bit of grease from her fingers.

I wait for the moment I can tuck myself away before zipping my pants again. She's in so much trouble. No matter how good that felt, she can't do shit like this. I won't die in a place like this. She may be used to the death and destruction inside walls like these, but I'm not. And I'm not willing to lose my life for emptying my balls in her hand. Maybe her pussy, but not her hand.

CHAPTER EIGHTEEN

Isabella

I drop my face to my fist as we pass familiar areas, and Vance remains silent on the drive home. His lips are drawn tight in a frown, and I'm surprised he's not in a better mood. He got to get off, unlike me.

"That was stupid, Bella. You know that, right?" he finally says.

I shrug. "No one noticed anything. Relax."

His dark eyes jump to mine. "Yeah, but if they had, we'd both be dead. Why is being a dirty fucking girl worth more to you than your life? Or my life."

My eyes narrow. "Because I don't want to make my future husband come. I want to make *you* come."

"You think I didn't want to slip my hand up your skirt and fuck you with my fingers until you came in front of your future family? But I didn't, because I'm old enough to realize that I can do that for you at home, when we aren't in a place with far more guns than I have on me."

I scoff. "I'm not a child, Vance. I'm old enough to realize

it too. But I *needed* to put my hand on you. The flame of jealousy in your eyes drove me crazy."

I wanted his jealousy to pour out of him and onto my hand. The frustrating pleasure on his face made me hunger for his come.

Not mine.

His.

"You wait till we get home, little girl. I'll show you the real definition of need."

His words make my mouth gape. He sure knows how to say things that make me a sopping wet mess. My mind goes to him between my legs, to his expert tongue licking at my clit. It makes me want to tug my panties aside and fuck myself with my fingers to calm the ache.

We pull into the underground garage at my house. Vance still looks irritated, but there's something more in his expression as well. Something feral.

He walks around the car and opens my door. The intensity in his dark eyes makes me uncomfortable, but his menacing smirk only excites me. Warm breath rolls over my neck as he leans toward my ear.

"Go inside, and by the time I'm in there, you better have your panties off. Do you understand?"

My eyes round. "Yes, daddy," I whisper.

He can't touch me in this garage—there are cameras everywhere—and the tremble to his hands says he's fighting the urge to do exactly that.

I walk across the garage and head inside. I don't hear him following, but I know he will. When I close the door behind me, the familiar scent of home welcomes me. The silence, however, is far from familiar.

I raise the hem of my dress and slip off my panties, then I open the door again and hang the black fabric on the outside doorknob before closing it once more.

Where the hell is he?

I pour myself some red wine and sit at the island, growing impatient with each sip. He's taking his sweet time because it's mental foreplay. He knows I'm thinking about what he'll do to me with every aching breath as I sit in my kitchen, pantyless and alone.

The door finally opens and slams, and his overbearing form fills the room. A tight expression pinches his face, but he pulls his hand from his pocket, opening his fingers to reveal my panties in his grasp. When he smirks, I know I'm in for it.

He makes his way across the kitchen in record time, taking my hair and balling it into his fist, then stuffing my panties into my mouth. The taste of my wetness slides across my tongue.

"Such a bad girl, Bella. You know that, right?"

I breathe through my nose, throwing him a quick nod. I *am* a bad girl. If I wasn't, I wouldn't be trying to get my rocks off with my bodyguard.

He puts himself between my thighs, my dress riding up and bunching against my hips. His hand drops between us, and he puts his warm fingers against my bare skin. An electrical bolt of energy pulls a gasp past my lips, and I nearly swallow my damn underwear.

Vance leans into me, burying his face in the crook of my neck. "I've never needed to make someone come as much as I need to make you come right now. I want to feel you around my hand so I can imagine it was my cock instead."

He pushes two fingers inside me and stretches me before he fills me up to his knuckles. Before I can gasp again, he pulls the panties from my mouth and silences me as his lips spread on mine in a fiery kiss.

Even though his lips are just on my mouth, I feel them everywhere else. My skin lights on fire as he pulls out and plunges inside me again, harder and faster with every thrust. He ingests my moans, taking them inside him and swallowing them.

I tilt my pelvis to grant him better access, and it sends him just a fraction deeper. A strong, almost painful feeling blooms deep inside me. I whimper against his mouth, and he inhales those sounds, too.

He's showing me the true definition of need, just like he promised. He selfishly fucks me with his fingers, ignoring my pain as he forces pleasure from me.

"Have you ever squirted before?" he asks, drawing his lips away enough to let my breath escape and dance along his words.

"No," I whisper. I don't think I could, anyway. It seems like something they do in porn and shit. Not real life.

"Another first I can take?" he growls. "Grip me with your hands."

This seems dramatic, but I listen to him, mostly because his hand is buried inside my pussy and I don't want it to stop. I grip the sleeves of his suit jacket, and he fucks me harder, faster, and deeper than I ever thought I could handle.

The growing heat in my gut erupts, and I'm overtaken by an intense urge to bare down on his fingers. I draw my abdomen in, and the pressure intensifies. To put out the fire inside me, Vance pulls his fingers from me and releases a gush of liquid. An intense orgasm washes over me, extinguishing any blaze that remained after what just exploded down the front of Vance's pants.

I've never felt such a thing. I'm squealing like a pig being slaughtered, I know that, but I have no control of the sounds I'm making or the quaking of my body. As unattractive as I feel, Vance seems to love it.

"Good fucking girl," he says, and it soothes the waves inside me, leaving a calm surface.

"Will you please fuck me?" I beg.

I need more. That force from his hand is something I could never mimic myself, not even with toys. I want to feel that strength inside me. I want his cock to rearrange my insides even more than his fingers did.

Vance smiles down at me, and I know it's a no. I can see it on his face. But he loves that I asked.

He loves that I begged for it.

"You know I can't fuck you. I'm already way outside of my job description with my hand buried inside you like this."

Fuck his job description. Where is it? I'll rewrite it to say *Keep Isabella happy at all costs, even if that means fucking her senseless before she gets married to an asshole.*

CHAPTER NINETEEN

Vance

Oh boy. I am slipping straight to hell with this girl. I worked too hard to getting into this business to fuck my way out of it now, but with her sleeping beside me, fully satiated from her orgasms last night, it's hard to remember my self-imposed policy against having sex with my clients.

Technically . . . her father is my client, not her.

No, I remind myself. I can't get inside her on a technicality like that. She's an extension of him. She's my fucking client too.

Besides, her wedding is in what? Three days? Which means I'll be dragged to all their events and shit, even if they don't want me there. There won't be time to fuck daddy's little princess on his dime.

"Hey." She stirs, arching her back and pushing her ass into my thigh.

I shake my head because she doesn't quit. From her first blink in the morning to the last at night, the girl thinks only of sex. Men don't even think about it as much as her; I'm convinced of it.

"Why are you up this early?" I ask. I haven't really slept. I think I dozed off for a few hours. *Maybe.*

"Rehearsal today. Don't you remember? I told you about it."

See? Fucking events. I think I'd remember if she told me that. Or maybe she mentioned it while I was blinded by horniness, which also makes me deaf, I guess.

"You didn't tell me that," I say, sticking to my guns on that. I'd remember if she'd said we had to be in front of her husband again.

Because God, I want to shoot him square in the face. Not even because she's marrying him, but because he's everything I hate about their world. The fact that they marry off people the way they do is fucking weird.

"Don't you know how weddings work?" she asks, sitting up in bed.

"Consensual ones? Yeah. Whatever this shit is? No."

I HELP her out of the car at the venue. My eyes catch on her, even though I saw her before we left. The falling sun's orange rays explode over her and mix with the vibrant red of her dress. She's stunning. I adjust the cuffs of my suit and rip my eyes from her before the family notices.

Isabella hooks her arm in mine, and we ascend the long walkway to a home which belongs to neither family. Staff meets us indoors and brings us to the backyard. Well, court-yard. Everything is surrounded by fancy mansion walls except this huge yard. So green and lush. It's like stepping into the fucking rainforest.

A tall wedding arch draped in sparkles and fabric stands in the center. I'm pretty sure it's decorated with actual diamonds. A walkway leads right to the ostentatious thing.

My eyes scan the area and land on the long table. Somehow it's expensive features still look like they belong beside the fucking Amazon. Two thrones—that's literally all I can describe them as—sit at the far end. For Mr. and Mrs., I'm sure.

God, it's infuriating. My first marriage was in the damn courthouse with a very inconvenienced judge. Our divorce was in front of the same judge. Something tells me these people don't divorce.

Her husband-to-be walks up and takes her from my arm with visible hatred. I really don't belong here, and he makes sure I know it. I feel like I belong here more than him, but whatever.

I sit down at the table with a strong fucking drink as I wait for the rest of the party to join us. Family shit I'm not meant to be privy to, I guess. They shouldn't worry. I don't want to be privy to shit.

Finally, the family comes together, and those who weren't at the last dinner look at me with a who-the-fuck-is-this-guy expression.

"This is Vance, the one I hired to watch over my little angel before her big day. Didn't want anything coming between this union," her father says to some confused faces.

The best part is *I'm* the one who could really get between this union by letting myself get between her legs. But that's neither here nor there.

Her husband scoffs. His brother scoffs louder. I down my drink and demand another as soon as those two take their places at the head of the table. In their fucking thrones.

I rub my finger along the rim of my glass and zone out as they talk about the intricacies of the ceremony. If I look at them, I'll get homicidal. I know it. I can feel it. Even his red tie matches her dress.

They fucking *match*.

"I've always wanted an outdoor wedding, ever since I was a kid. Right, Daddy?" Isabella looks at her father, but the word makes my spine snap to attention. She's saying it with the same dripping sensuality that she does at home.

Jesus, girl, not here. Not fucking here. I had to give up my gun at the door, and I'm sure none of them have given up theirs.

"It's . . ." Antonio slaps a bug off the table and throws his drink down like a petulant child. "It's not what I want. I would rather have it in my living room than out here."

"It's one day," his father says, trying to soothe him. "Happy wife, happy life, Tony. You'll learn that quickly."

The whole table laughs. Except me. These people are insufferable. Antonio is a baby. The wedding is dramatic and overly extravagant. But Isabella is right. It *is* beautiful out here.

Antonio drops his head into his hand. I want to reach over and strangle him. He's acting like he's getting married in a two-star hotel. Gasp.

My eyes meet hers, and both families disappear. It's me beside her instead of her husband. I imagine fucking her throat while I sit on that damn throne. Staring down at something as beautiful as the landscape out here. More so, even.

She throws me a flirty smirk, and my vision fills with the dicks around me again. The distance between us widens as I'm thrown back in my seat.

It's at that moment that I realize how much I wish I could be the one beside her. And that sucks.

CHAPTER TWENTY

Isabella

Vance and I sit across from each other at home. A drink sits in front of him, and it seems as if he takes heavy swigs every minute. When the glass is empty, I go and pour him some more.

My wedding is tomorrow. That means this job is over for him after tonight. Neither of us knows what to say about it.

I saw how he looked at me at the rehearsal. The hungry frustration in his eyes and the need to kill my fiancé written all over his face. Kill him for *me*.

When my father first brought Vance into my home, I was annoyed—angry, even—that he thought I needed a babysitter. Now I don't want to be without him. The world seems daunting whenever I peek from beneath his wing. But he isn't one of us. He's not someone I would ever be allowed to be with.

I finish pouring his drink, set down the bottle, and climb onto his lap. No words pass between us as I wrap my arms around his neck. He keeps his hands on the table. He's being distant, and he needs to be. I know that.

"Daddy," I whisper, nuzzling my face into his neck, where the coarse hairs rub my cheeks.

He sighs. "Don't, little girl. I'm not in the mood."

"It's our last day together."

"I know," he whispers.

"We still have time to fuck, you know. You don't have to hand me off to Antonio as the pure queen he thinks I'll be."

Vance shakes his head. "Yes, I do."

I stop nuzzling him. "What's a bigger fuck-you than screwing me the night before I get married?"

A drawn-out sigh leaves Vance's lips. "If you asked me day one if I'd want to do a fuck-you to you *and* your husband-to-be, I'd have jumped all over it. But now, fucking you would do nothing but break my own heart."

His words drip with a sad frustration, and I feel it too. In my bones. I've grown so attached to him. He's given me so many firsts. I truly feel like he'd dive in front of a bullet for me, which is more than my husband would ever do. Nerves flutter around my belly with large, nauseating wings.

I straighten and look into his eyes. I would do anything short of giving up my name to be with him and even then, if I had a paper in front of me that released me from the Vendetti family name, I'd be tempted to sign it.

I lean in and kiss him. His lips don't spread on mine, and a hardness comes over his eyes before he pulls away from me. He nearly knocks me onto the floor as he pushes me off and stands.

"Please don't make this harder than it already is," he says, his usually strong and confident tone wavering.

"But—"

"But nothing. I'm going to my room. Stay out of it. Don't

come into my bed. I'm not kidding. Have a good fucking wedding tomorrow."

"Please don't be like this, Vance," I beg, taking a step toward him, despite his harsh glare.

He throws his hands up. "What else could I be like? I fell for you, and that's absolutely suicidal of me. I don't want to do my job. I don't want to protect you and keep you pure and innocent. I want to take you in ways you couldn't even handle and never let you go to your wedding. If killing him meant I could be with you, he'd be dead already."

His admission takes me aback, but I keep silent and allow him to continue.

"But even if he was six feet underground, they wouldn't allow you to be with me," he says. "It's hard for me to be in the same room as you without feeling the suffocating truth in that. Being inside you would only make it worse. It would kill me."

Before I can offer a rebuttal for the words surging from his mouth, he turns and walks down the hall.

My heart fractures in my chest as I realize the truth in every single thing he's said. I've fallen for him too. Somewhere along the way, chasing his dick became chasing his heart instead. But he's right. I can't marry outside the prominent families, and especially not my bodyguard. The suggestion alone would probably get him killed.

Maybe both of us.

The door down the hall slams and makes me jump out of my skin. I wish he understood that I share his desperate frustration. It's not just about getting my pussy wet, it's about getting it wet for him. With him.

He's who I feel safe with, and I want him to be my first. I understand how that complicates things, but can't men just turn it off? Fuck some strange without worrying about anyone's feelings? Can't he do that for me?

I head toward my room but stop and look down the hall, staring at his door as if he might come out and change his mind and fuck me out of hatred for my family. My husband. This situation.

But he doesn't. Silence comes from his side of the door.

I'm so tempted to go into his room instead of my own, but he was so sure of himself with every word.

Stay out of it.

I force myself to listen. I go into my room with an emptiness in my heart that will never be filled by my husband, no matter how often he has sex with me. I get undressed and climb into bed. The cool sheets embrace me in a tight hug, and I imagine they're Vance's hands wrapping around me, smoothing my skin as his fingers race over my body.

I lift the sheet away and bring my hand between my legs. My fingertips dance along my skin before I put them on my slit. I rub through my lips until my clit swells. I imagine the fingers are Vance's instead of my own. I remember how he touched me before, and it makes my chest rise from the bed.

A knock at the door startles me, and I rip my hand away.

"Don't touch yourself, Isabella. You know the rules. The game's ending, but it's not over."

My eyes leap to the camera. I assumed he wasn't watching me anymore. Not since we've been sleeping together in the same bed. But this scolding means he's still got his eye on me. And he still got jealous.

"Make me obey the rules, then," I say, a flirty hint in my voice.

His steps recede from the other side of the door, heading back toward his room. I wrap myself in the sheet again and turn over with a huff.

Women dream about weddings like these, and I did too . . . until I started dreaming about someone like Vance instead. But he's right about everything. There can be no *us*, no matter how much either of us wants it.

CHAPTER TWENTY-ONE

Vance

Despite being back in my own home, I feel like I'm in a foreign land. It feels like I don't belong here anymore. I now hate the familiar decor, like the oversized recliner standing in the corner of the room. It doesn't hold a candle to the leather chair in Isabella's house, especially when she sat on my lap. Everything just seems miserable here.

Without her.

As much as she drove me nuts—literally insane—being without her feels like I've had a limb forcibly removed from my body. One minute I had a happiness I've never felt, and the next, I was sitting in my quiet home, hating everything about it. And myself.

I look at the clock. The big, beautiful wedding is set for today, and it will fulfill all her dreams and her father's fucking wishes. The hands move toward four p.m., inching closer to the grand event at five-thirty. The seconds crawl along, torturing me.

Actually, I think I'd rather be physically tortured than sit here and deal with the mental anguish from knowing my girl is about to give herself to someone else.

My girl? She's not my girl.

I remind myself that a woman like Isabella wouldn't have let me sniff in her general direction before I got this gig. She doesn't want me. She only feels an insatiable lust for the man who was in close proximity. It could have been anyone.

I have to let her go.

I'm trying. I'm really trying. If I wasn't, I wouldn't have let her go to the wedding in the first place. I would have killed the man who came to take her to the massive mansion.

As stupid as that decision would have been, it took everything in me to keep from doing exactly that. I had to remind myself to keep my feet planted because I was one word away from digging my own grave. I should have killed him for silently standing in her living room while wearing sunglasses *indoors* like a moron. Or for standing in the home that had begun to feel like *my* home too.

She shot me a look before she went with him. I probably imagined it, but that look seemed as if she was fighting her own urges to run into my arms and never look back. I had to bite back everything I felt and give her a reassuring nod because I didn't know what would have happened if I didn't.

She had to go. She has to get married. But I can't stop these homicidal thoughts from racing through my mind.

I want to string up every man involved in this fiasco by the balls, starting with her father. I'd fight the entire fucking family if it meant I could keep her from marrying someone else. But that's not realistic. That's suicide.

I hope her father is happy. I hope everything is to his fucking liking. His perfect business model is falling into place, regardless of what Isabella wants or needs. And what she wants and needs isn't that fucker she's marrying.

My head drops to my fist. Memories of that girl wrap

around my chest and squeeze, suffocating me. Her touch. The way she sounded when she laughed. When she was playful and coaxed some of that out of me as well.

I want that.

I need it.

And I can't fucking have it.

But what if I could?

My back stiffens, and I sit up again. What if I didn't go in with my guns blazing like some kind of low-budget Rambo? I could take out some of the men if I had to. Some, but not all. That's why it's suicide. This isn't a movie. But what if I snuck in, quiet as a fucking church mouse, and made sure she left with me?

The thoughts renew something inside me. I get up, change out of my pajamas, and put on a crisp pair of slacks and a pressed shirt. I don't fully suit up, but I throw my jacket over my shoulder and whip open my gun safe.

My faithful pistol begs to be chosen, so I slide it into my holster. But I'll need more than one. I tuck a second handgun down the back of my pants. Metal clinks together as I slip the 9mm magazines into my pocket.

I consider wearing armor, but if it gets to that point, I'm better off dead than in the hands of their families. I'd rather bleed out than allow them to decide my fate. Which—spoiler alert—would be much worse than dying.

I get in my car, which isn't nearly as flashy as the luxury cars that will surely fill the valet parking area at the event. I'll stick out like a sore thumb.

A smile creeps across my face at my own ingenuity when I get an idea. If I take Isabella's BMW, I'll blend in with the big money. As much as I'd never want to be like these fucks, I need to be like them today.

I crank up the radio to drown my bickering thoughts, but it doesn't do much good. The closer I get to Isabella's family home, the more my chest tightens. I fear I'm having a coronary as my heart thuds against my sternum like a galloping cavalry.

When I reach her side of the house, I enter using the spare key I made when I assumed Isabella would cause more problems than she ultimately did. I snatch her BMW keyring off the hook beside the door and head toward the garage.

The bright fluorescent lights spring to life as I enter the concrete showroom. And that's essentially what this garage is. The cars that take up this space are hardly driven. What a waste of fucking money.

I bypass the sporty options and head straight for the sleek BMW at the far end. I drop into the driver's seat, grip the steering wheel with one hand, and press the ignition with the other. Looking at the dashboard clock as I back out of the garage, I give myself one more chance to stop this insanity. Is it really worth the risk I plan to take?

Fuck yeah, it is. I press the gas a little harder.

She's worth the pending mayhem and the war I'll wage if we make it out of there alive. She's worth all of it. But I'm not sure I'm worth the same to her or if she'd betray her family to remain by my side. Will she give it all up for me? I don't have all that much to lose, but she has everything.

I guess we'll see, because I'm about to fuck around and find out.

CHAPTER TWENTY-TWO

Isabella

My future husband waits just outside, and my stomach is in my throat. I'd rather receive a hot sauce enema twice a day for the rest of my life than walk down an aisle toward him.

But I have no choice.

Any illusion of a choice vanished when I looked back at Vance, pleading with my eyes as the Vendettis' security prepared to haul me away. He only threw me a casual smile and dropped his gaze. I thought there was more between us than that. I clearly saw something that wasn't there.

Someone knocks, and my father's jovial voice creeps through the door and mocks me. It's time. My life is fucking over and he's as happy as can be. Why doesn't *he* marry Antonio if he thinks it's such a good idea?

I open the door and he takes me into his arms and plants an alcohol-infused kiss on my cheek. Instead of hiding the despair on my face, I wear it like a badge. I want him to see it. It won't make a difference—feelings don't belong in this business—but I refuse to don my plastic smile before I have to.

"Don't fuck this up," he says with a gentle smack of my cheek.

I want to scream that this is already fucked up. An asteroid is headed straight for my world, and nothing can stop the impending destruction. But what does it matter now? A nuke already decimated the entire population of my heart when Vance let me go instead of fighting for me.

I know my worth. I deserve to be fought for.

My father holds out his arm, and I slide my hand into the crook of his elbow like the dutiful daughter I am. Birds twitter above our heads as we step into the courtyard. It sounds more like a dirge to me—a sorrowful lamentation for the loss of all that I am and all that I could have been. This is the day I lay my hopes and dreams to rest. A black dress would better match my mood than this white lie I wear.

Pink rose petals wilt under my strappy heels as I stand at the head of the center aisle and spot Antonio. A tight frown tugs at the corners of his thin lips, even once he sees me. He swats at a group of gnats dive-bombing his sweaty face.

I look away from him and study the two very different families drawn together by money and greed. Two groups of people willing to sell me off to the highest bidder. I am the prize heifer being led to slaughter.

My feet long to turn in the opposite direction and carry me away from this nightmare, but I will them forward. Memories of Vance flash and flicker with every step I take on that petal-strewn path. His eyes. His smirk. The way he touches me. The ways I want him to touch me.

My thoughts wrap around Vance, cradling him and keeping his memory safe. His face is the only one I see until my father releases my arm and gives me to the man who doesn't deserve me.

Antonio's eyes lock on my tits. He isn't concerned with the effort a team of people put into my hair and makeup. He only cares that my boobs are elevated to high heaven. Usually, I like it when a man appreciates my assets, but not right now. Right now, I hate it. Vance always looked me in my eyes before eye-fucking me.

I zone out as the family priest drones on about the importance and sanctity of marriage. I pretend I'm anywhere else. Being burned alive would be less painful than this.

When the priest asks if Antonio accepts me as his wife, he says, "Yep." That's how invested he is. The priest has to encourage him to say a proper "I do."

"And Isabella, do you take Antonio Vendetti to be your wedded husband? Do you promise to love him, comfort him, honor and keep him, for better or worse, for richer or poorer, in sickness and health and, forsaking all others, be faithful only to him for so long as you both shall live?"

The two simple words stick in my throat like chewed gum on hot pavement. Antonio's eyes narrow.

So I force out the words. "I do."

I do not. How the fuck can I forsake all others when all I want is another?

We exchange rings, and the priest gives us the command to kiss. I do my duty and remain in place as Antonio leans toward me, but I'm screaming inside. His greedy hands grip my hips and pull me closer. His poisonous lips paint mine with sludge as his cold, sluggish tongue tries to pry its way into my mouth. I pull away, refusing what I can while I can. When he takes me to our marital bed tonight, I will no longer have the voice to say no.

The journey down the aisle and the family photography session are a blur. I feel as if I've just received a terminal diagnosis and I'm running on autopilot. Breathing and nodding. That's all I can do.

When we sit for our meal in the reception area, I pick at my food and imagine Vance beside me, also picking at his food because he'd be as miserable as I am right now if he were here. But he's not.

After having him by my side for so long, I feel as if I've lost a part of myself. I grip my tongue between my teeth and bite down to keep from crying.

Antonio jabs my thigh beneath the table. "Can you at least pretend you're happy to be my wife?" he whispers.

I flash the best smile I can muster, pick up a forkful of filet mignon, and shove it into my mouth before I can tell him how I really feel.

Also, fuck him. It's an arranged marriage. Not everyone feels joy when forced to marry someone they didn't choose for themselves. Even when both parties are excited about the situation, there are still awkward moments and misery to be had.

Fuck, I hate this. I almost wish I'd never met Vance. If my heart didn't know what it was missing, I could have at least looked forward to getting laid for the first time. Now I want to avoid that moment completely.

I'm a vegan who craves a juicy steak, but I'm forced to sit in front of a plate of limp asparagus for the rest of my life. I glance at Antonio and feel a twinge of guilt for my thoughts. Limp asparagus is a bit harsh. For the asparagus.

I've secretly hoped Vance would swoop in and save me from this ordeal, but I think it's time to acknowledge the facts. My dark knight won't be riding in to carry me away to safety. I am alone on this battlefield, caught in a war that is not of my making. I have fallen on the sword for my family, and now I only have to lie down and die. The birds were right to sing a dirge. This is my funeral.

CHAPTER TWENTY-THREE

Vance

The clock on the dash ticks onward with each mile, long surpassing the appointed time of the wedding. I couldn't get near the mansion in time to stop the ceremony. Now I'm left to drive back and forth along this road in front of the mansion, my blood rising another ten degrees with every pass.

I've lost her for good. She's married off to that fucking asshole, and there's nothing I can do about it.

It's time to give up and admit I've been beaten. This isn't an easy task for a driven man like me, but I pull onto a side road and turn around to go back home. It's the smart thing to do. I was never meant to be with a woman like Bella.

Weight in my right foot keeps me planted on the brakes. Something inside me claws to the surface, begging me to be irrational and wild. To find her. To make sure she's truly gone and that there's no hope of making her mine. I shouldn't listen to that voice inside my head, but it's so loud. It screams over any logical thought, forcing its way to the forefront and waving a banner that I can't see around. It fills my vision in a blaze of red.

I watch the mansion through the trees, waiting as a crowd of people and their respective security begin to disperse. Each family has their own bodyguard that would give their life for their safety, just as I would have done for Isabella.

Just as I would still do for her. My life is hers alone.

I put the car in park. I can't leave without her. Unless she tells me to get out of her life, I refuse to give up on her. I never should have allowed them to take her away. Not without asking how she feels about me first. Now the question gnaws at my heart, tearing away pieces until I no longer feel it beating.

By the time the sun dips beneath the horizon, the security has diminished to a trickle. The big mansion on the hill is less protected now. If I plan to do this, it's now or never.

I remove my gun from its leather holster and pull back the slide, making sure it's still loaded and operational. When it clicks into place, the decision is made. I'll find her and give her the chance to come with me. I'd rather die than be without her, so who cares if I risk my life now?

I pull out my GPS and plot a path through back roads that will deliver me to the back of the mansion.

This luxury vehicle was made for city streets, not dirt roads and potholes, but it cuts through the red dirt with ease. Even though I'm moving at a slow pace, a plume of dust rises around the car. I can only hope the loosely packed dirt gives way to pavement when I'm closer to the mansion. I'd hate to give away my position.

Still, I struggle to keep my foot from pressing on the gas pedal. I need to reach her before he gets his fucking hands on her. Before he takes what's mine. Even if he owns her pussy by marriage, I claimed and marked her before he did.

Watching the GPS, I bring the car to a stop on the side of

the road. These woods run right up to the edge of the property. My destination isn't far off now, and I can only hope I'm not heading toward my grave.

I'm fairly certain I know where she'll be; she pointed out the window overlooking the garden when we were last here and told me that's where she'd finally lose her virginity. She said it to annoy me, and it worked. She didn't realize she was giving me the information I would need today.

To save her.

To save myself.

I get out of the car, then holster one pistol and sink the other beneath my waistband before I disappear into the forest. Thick brush grips my ankles, and the trees crowd each other like tourists in Times Square. Branches reach for my face, stretching spindly fingers toward my cheeks, but I dodge out of their way as I race toward the mansion.

Nothing will stop me from getting to her now. A rattlesnake could sink its hollow fangs into my leg and I would just keep going.

The sun has gone to bed, wrapping the world in darkness. Owls hoot within the treetops, and animals scurry through the brush, seeking safety from the predators. But I can't pay attention to any of that. I think only of planning my uninvited entrance into their home. The guard stations were vacant the night of the party, but I'm certain they're inhabited now, especially after such a toxic union. Everyone will be on high alert.

It doesn't matter. I'll send a bullet through the skull of anyone who dares to stand between me and Isabella. Mark my words, blood will paint my hands tonight, though I don't know if it will pour from a guard or if it will stain the sheets beneath Isabella when I take her the way she always begged for me to.

Fuck, I should have given in to her. I should have cast

aside that stupid little rule I made for myself. I thought sleeping with her would complicate things, but look at everything now. It's complicated as fuck, and I still never experienced her perfection wrapped around my cock.

A sprawling courtyard waits just beyond the shadows of this tree line. The guard booth illuminates a small square in the grass, and a guard lingers inside. A spotlight scans the landscape. Dodging the circle of illumination, I make my way across the lawn until I'm behind the booth. Dark hair swivels as the guard scans the multitude of security cameras. He must have spotted something, because he studies a frame a little longer than the others.

He must have spotted . . . me.

I rip open the metal door, and he whips around to face me, eyes wide with shock. His hand rises to the radio. I grab it from him before he can alert anyone.

As much as I would love to pull out my gun and blow his head off—it would certainly be the fastest way to finish this— it would be too loud. Guards would flock to this location like flies on shit. And we can't have that, can we?

I grip his wrist and twist until I hear something snap. Before he can scream, I duck behind him and press my hand over his mouth. With my free hand, I grip the radio's stiff cable and wind it around his neck, releasing his mouth in the process. He can't scream if he can't breathe.

I tighten my hold on the cord and watch as his face deepens to red before going a sickly shade of purple. Blood vessels crawl along his scleras and spread like spiderwebs. Then they burst. Red fireworks become a flood encircling his irises. His hands flail, scrabbling for me, but I won't be deterred. I won't stop until he is one less obstacle between me and Isabella.

When his hands still at his sides and a river of piss runs

down his leg and splatters onto the concrete floor, I know he's dead.

I settle him in the chair and prop his head so that it looks as if he's watching the security monitors. If anyone happens to come by, it won't look suspicious. Well, as long as they don't study him too closely. Living people blink.

I pull the keyring from his waist and leave the booth. After a short jaunt across the courtyard, I let myself inside Antonio's home.

His sanctuary will soon become an abattoir, and he is the beast I plan to slaughter. I'll decide how he dies once I know if he's touched her. If he's already defiled her, I might have to make it very slow and very painful.

As I approach the door, adrenaline buzzes through me in a rush. Questions burn through my brain. And it's time to get answers.

CHAPTER TWENTY-FOUR

Isabella

Glass shatters against the floor, and another explosion of sound whooshes by my head. Even though anxiety jolts through my body, I refuse to show it.

I raise my chin and harden my gaze as Antonio storms closer. Fiery hatred blazes in his eyes; it isn't the sort of look I'd expect from my husband. We appear to be equally enthused about this arrangement.

To be fair, he was plenty enthused about owning me before he saw me with Vance at the dinner. Now he believes I've been defiled before our wedding night.

I wish. If Vance had given in and taken my purity like I'd begged him to, this torment would almost be worth it.

He steps into me, and his warm, liquor-laced breath rolls over my chest as he pushes me against the wall. I raise my chin higher. I refuse to cow to him and become some lowly subordinate who bends to his every will and desire.

If his type is a compliant woman, I'm not it. I'm mouthy. Opinionated. Dare I say, bitchy? I have no intention of changing who I am for the betterment of either of our families. Not even if it would better myself.

"Miserable. Fucking. Bitch," he snaps, a drunken slur stretching out every word. "My father warned me about you."

I curl my lip. "I'm glad my reputation precedes me."

His fist slams beside my head, and a hairline crack spreads across the marble wall. "This is what I mean!"

I flash my dark eyes up at him. "Fuck you."

His tan hand rushes toward my scalp, and he winds his fingers through my hair, snatching back my head before bringing me toward his chest. "You are worth much less than you think you are, Isabella. This union makes just as much sense if you end up dead. Maybe even more so. If you're out of the picture, I get the benefits without having to suffer through the disgust of having a whore for a wife."

My eyes narrow on him as I strain against his grasp. "Care to fucking elaborate on how a virgin can be a whore?"

He releases a deep, mocking laugh. "I have doubts that you're still a virgin, *Mrs.* Vendetti. Especially after I saw the way you look at that fucking guard of yours. I never expected a girl like you to cream over the help."

I one hundred percent creamed over the help. Came for him, even. Came *to* him. But I didn't consider him "the help." Those words never rolled off my tongue with such disgust.

"You sound jealous of him, *husband.* Worried you can't live up to the expectations you've fabricated between your three brain cells?"

That does it. I've emasculated him to the very core of his being. He would never be jealous of someone like Vance in any other circumstance, but he is now. Even if he socks his fist into my cheek to tell himself differently, he can't deny the truth.

I stand without flinching as he draws his hand back to hit me, but before he drives his knuckles into my face, he stops.

He must have remembered the honeymoon we'll leave for in the morning. It would look really shitty if his new bride had a giant bruise on her beautiful face as she lounged on the beach. His hand strangles my dark hair, and he leans closer.

"Show me you aren't a whore," he snarls in my ear.

Show him how? By being exactly that? No thanks. I'm good.

"I have a headache," I quip, motioning toward the hand shaking my head.

It's pathetic. A month ago, I dreamed about what it would be like to fuck someone. Anyone. A week ago, I begged Vance to make that dream a reality. I literally got on my knees and pleaded for him to take my virginity. That's how desperate I was.

But now? I'd do anything to avoid it.

My heart aches when I think of Vance. My soul bleeds. I don't want to lose my virginity anymore, because I've finally realized it shouldn't be given away so freely. It's meant for one person, and he isn't here.

Gripping my hair, Antonio yanks me toward the bed and heaves me onto the mattress. I land on my back, and he crawls between my legs. His hands work their way beneath my dress despite each furious kick I aim at him.

My hands grip his wrists as they unzip his slacks. A look replaces the mask on his face that was already so foreign to me. He doesn't care if I want this. *He* wants it, and that's all that matters.

This isn't how this was supposed to be. I wanted to give away this part of me, not have it wrenched from my unwilling grasp. But now this part of me is no longer mine to give away. It belongs to someone else. It belongs to . . .

Vance.

Tears heat the backs of my eyes, and my sinuses burn. I never cry. I *never* fucking cry. I scream reminders in my head.

Don't show him your tears! Don't ever show a man those little glass balls of weakness, because fuck them! They don't deserve them!

There's only *one* person I would shed tears for. And it's not the man between my legs. I will cry for the man who rescued me from myself on several occasions. I will cry for the man who saw through my tough exterior and found the person buried within. But I refuse to shed a single tear for anyone else.

"Look at me, whore," Antonio growls, his hand prodding between my legs as he snatches my panties aside.

Memories of Vance blanket my mind, soothing the panic raging through my bones. I think of him. His strong, hungry hands on my body. The way he looked at me as if he needed me as much as I needed him.

Heat burns against my crotch, and I know what's coming. I look up at the ceiling. I look anywhere but at the man who is about to destroy me.

Antonio draws back his hips, and I clutch the sheet in my hands, closing my eyes so I can hide from the monster. I squeeze the thin fabric, grit my teeth, and prepare for the hell barreling toward me.

Cold vacancy slips between us, and his hands move off my legs. My eyes open. He's ripped away from me, and I scream.

I draw my legs together, pinching them closed, and shield myself from the mayhem erupting around me. Grunts float between my ears. Cloth rips, flesh collides with flesh, and feet squeak against the floor. My spine stiffens and I jerk my head toward the sounds that seem to come from everywhere and nowhere all at once.

My eyes are fucking deceiving me. Antonio must have knocked me out, and now I'm dreaming. I pinch my arm to be sure, and the sharp sting tells me I'm very much awake. And I'm very much watching Antonio get the living hell beaten out of him.

The man pummeling my husband could kill him much more quickly if he wanted to, but he doesn't. He's toying with him. And he's doing it while his dark eyes fuck me with a hot, jealous glare.

As he squeezes my husband's throat and stops his onslaught, his warm, buttery voice permeates me to my very core. "Did you miss me, little girl?"

CHAPTER TWENTY-FIVE

Vance

Her husband's fight dissipates in my grasp. Bella's expression hardens. She looks as though she doesn't believe what she sees in front of her. As her lips tighten into a hard line and her eyes widen with uncertainty, I can't help but wonder how this will turn out.

Will she run into my arms? Or will she run away from me?

She says nothing, but then the corners of her lips draw upward in the most intoxicating smirk.

"Kill him," she whispers.

I planned to do it anyway, but hearing those sadistic words roll from her pretty mouth fills my head with a dizzying euphoria.

The words have the opposite effect on Antonio. He goes into a blind panic, renewing his fight. He flails against me, gripping my hands and pushing off the wall in a pathetic attempt to break free. Everything about him is pathetic.

Her dark eyes flash up at me, and she climbs out of bed and comes toward me. She's a wildcat, stalking toward her prey. When she reaches the sniveling man in my grasp, she runs the back of her hand down his cheek.

"You are worth *so* much less than you think," she says, her lips pinching at the end. "Isn't that what you said to me? You must have been projecting because I'm clearly worth something to someone. Who has come to save you from this marriage, husband?"

He said that to her? My blood simmers to a boil. She's worth so much more than he ever deserved. More than I deserve.

She looks at me. "Turn him toward me."

I spin him around so that he faces her, then wrap my arm around his throat in a chokehold. She draws back her leg and knees him so hard in the nuts that I feel it in my own junk. Breath rushes from my lungs at the sheer force of the impact.

Her eyes meet mine again, and she gives me a quick nod. I don't need much more than that to know what she expects next.

I tighten my grip on Antonio's neck. Tighter. Tighter. I squeeze as he struggles against me, then he relaxes as the oxygen flees his brain. Though he's relaxed, I don't release him. I wait for that final push his body will make when he realizes the end is upon him.

The way a person fights when they stand at the precipice of death is something I can't explain. Then it happens. He bucks against me, clawing my hands until he breaks off a nail in my skin. His legs kick and scramble for an escape he won't find. Then they flail at nothing, slowing to weak jerks and jolts. Feeling his fight seep from his body is almost as euphoric as her homicidal words.

Antonio goes limp, and his hands drift to his sides, the fingers still curled in that desperate pose. I hold him for another minute, waiting for the violent and involuntary contractions in his chest that herald the final moments of death. When those gasping motions cease, I drop him to the floor and step over him.

I pull Isabella into me, and her lips meet mine with an intensity I don't expect—a hunger I thought I'd fabricated in my mind. No, this hunger is real, and she's shoving her tongue in my mouth like she's been thinking about it just as much as I have.

I moan into her mouth as her lips spread on mine. "Bella," I growl, fisting her dark hair in my hand. I never thought she'd be back in my grasp. Something I could touch again. Now I never want to let her go. "Will you come with me?"

"Wh-what?"

"Will you leave all this behind to run away with me?" I ask again.

My heart sinks in my chest as my fears take physical form on her face. Instead of a spirited look, an excitement at my proposition, she looks as if I just asked her to give me both her fucking kidneys. It's a look that strips the worth from the efforts I've made to reach her.

Her mouth opens and closes. "Vance . . ."

I grab her by the shoulders. "I didn't kill everyone standing between me and you to hear my name. I came for a yes. I came for *you*. All of you."

"You don't even know what you're asking! It's suicide to—"

"Then I'm suicidal, Isabella. I don't want to leave here without you."

Her lips tighten. "I've thought of no one but you since they took me away from my house. I thought of you as I struggled through that awful wedding. You got me through all of that." She points to the bed. "But you can't just *leave* a family like mine. Love isn't an out. The only way out is in a fucking coffin!"

"And I will put every single member of both of these families inside one if it means I can have you by my side." I take a deep breath. " I will do whatever it takes to have you."

Her eyes narrow. "And what if I don't willingly come with you? Will you just abduct me?"

A deep laugh vibrates my throat. "No, I won't. I'm saying that if you *choose* to come with me, I'll do anything in my power to protect you and keep you safe. I can't lose you again."

"Protect me? It won't be *me* who'll need protecting. My god, Vance, are you thinking with the right head here?"

A smirk tugs at my lips. Of course I am. Her tight little pussy hasn't had the opportunity to taint the head on my shoulders, because I haven't even been inside it yet.

I draw her lips close to mine. "Neither head guides this decision, little girl. This does."

I grip her hand and place it on my chest. My heart thumps against her palm, rabid for her. And I think it just might shatter if she tells me no.

"I'll leave you here if you want to stay. I won't throw you over my shoulder and take you away. It's not my style. I won't beg for your affection, either, but I'll ask for it. I'm asking for it now." I swallow. "Will you come with me and let me protect you the way I know how?"

She throws her hands into the air. "I don't know. I just—"

"Let me lay you on this bed and spread your thighs, little girl. Let my name be the only one you scream out."

She closes her mouth and stares at me, the wheels turning in her mind. This is my final plea. If she says no, I'll leave and never look back, taking only her memory with me. But if she says yes, I will fuck her in a way that ensures she'll never consider letting me go again.

CHAPTER TWENTY-SIX

Isabella

I can't run away with Vance. It would be suicide, for one or both of us. He doesn't understand. He's not from this world I live in. It's like a gang. You don't leave once you're inside, and being born into it is the most inside you can be.

But his breath washes over mine, grazing my chin as I turn away so I can think of something else besides the warmth of his body against me. Even with my husband's blood still staining his knuckles, I've never wanted anything more than to give in to him right now.

I roll my eyes up to his, finally meeting them. "Vance."

He swallows, his Adam's apple bobbing so hard I think he might choke on it if I tell him no. "Don't say no to me, little girl." His fingers wrap around my chin and draw me to his mouth.

But he doesn't get it.

"I don't know what to do, Vance," I whisper, which isn't entirely true.

I know what I *want* to do. I want to run away with him

and find true happiness far from the underside of my father's thumb. But what I want isn't enough in this case. We'd need a fucking army for it to be enough. The Vendetti family would catch and kill both of us. My father would let me live, but he'd force me to watch him kill Vance before dragging me home and locking me away for the rest of my life.

"Let me help you make up your mind." He lifts me into his arms and carries me to the bed. I don't fight him. As he lays me down, his hand searches beneath my dress and lands between my legs. He frowns. "You're soaked. Did he do this to you?"

I shake my head. Double fuck no. "Absolutely not."

He brings his fingers to his lips and licks them. "Something turned you on."

Yes, something did, but it wasn't the man I married.

"You. I was thinking about you when he tried to . . ." I point to my very dead husband, unable to formulate the rest of the sentence.

Vance's lips draw into the most sensual smirk, and I forget all the reasons we can't run away together. I can only think of this moment, right now, and the need rising inside me.

Then the tips of his front teeth bite into his lower lip, and that's all she wrote for me.

"Yes," I whisper.

I lean into him and capture his lips, and his tongue finds mine with a hunger that warms the wetness between my legs. It's as if this stupid fucking marriage never pulled us apart. We've picked up right where we left off, and we're racing toward what we've both denied ourselves for far too long.

His hand laces through my hair and pulls me into him. His heartbeat pounds against my chest, matching the rapid rhythm coursing through me. I inhale each of his exhales until I feel dizzy, every breath he takes becoming my own.

Vance's hand moves to my thigh, and he squeezes. Everything about his touch feels familiar. Like home.

"Did you think about what it would feel like to fuck me?" he growls against my lips. "When he touched you, did you think about my hands instead?"

A breath of panic leaves my lips at the thought of what almost happened before Vance saved me, but he comforts me with his mouth and I relax. I'm safe now. As long as his arms are around me, I fear nothing.

He rises to his feet in front of me. His belt buckle jingles as he works it open, and then his zipper follows. His hands drift up my thighs, raising my skirt higher, and he spreads my legs with a strong, painful grip on both legs. I'm so open for him, so vulnerable, and that sends a rope of panic around my throat. I can't breathe.

He senses this and lightens his touch, trailing his fingers over the goosebumps that have risen on my thighs. "You're right to be scared. My cock won't feel good at first. But when you relax and stretch around me, you'll be in heaven. I'll make sure of that."

The panic loosens its hold around my neck, and I draw a breath. He'll make me feel good, and I don't want my first time to be with anyone else. I want this—I want *him*—right now.

I nod.

He leans over me, and the heat of his dick presses against me. I nearly panic again, but I keep my composure. I'm better than this. I've been chasing this moment for years, and now it's right in front of me. The man I was meant to share this moment with is right in front of me. I have the opportunity to give my virginity to someone I actually like, and I can't ruin this.

Silky skin brushes my clit before he's at my entrance. His

tip rests against me, not even *inside* me, and I gasp. Embarrassing.

"Ready to be mine, little girl?" he asks.

I wish he wouldn't. Wondering what I need to be so *ready* for is stressing me out worse than if he just pushed inside me. But I only nod as he pulls me into him.

When he eases into me, I'm as tight to his body as possible. A sharp pain rockets through my pelvis and groin, and it feels as if he's tearing me in half. I can't help but scream out, but I don't tell him to stop. I just whimper through the pain he warned me about. Even through this burning ache, I focus on the thump of his heart against my temple, and it warms that feeling away.

Thump. Thump.

It's the sound and the feel of the immense pleasure I'm giving him—the background vocals to his feral, hungry groans. He sounds like a starved man who's been seated before a banquet. With each taste of the feast I offer him, he vocalizes his pleasure.

My sounds join his, my whimpers becoming moans as he thrusts. His strokes lengthen and deepen. He's reading me from the inside, increasing his tempo and depth as my body allows.

"God, you feel even better than I imagined." He releases me and draws back his hips. Looking down, his eyebrows pull together. "I made you bleed." His eyes drift up to mine. "Bound by blood, Isabella. You're mine."

His cock has ripped through me and made me bleed. He's forged a bond in blood that only rivals the genetic bond I share with my father. A moan strangles from my throat.

His hand reaches between us and rubs my sensitive clit. His expert touch tightens my abdomen as he draws pleasure from deep within me with every push and pull of his hips.

"Daddy," I cry out.

"Good girl. Come for me," he whispers before leaning down and kissing me. He swallows every moan he wrenches out of me.

His soft and gravelly words send me careering off my cliff, and I come for the first time with a cock stretching me and stuffing me until I feel more full than I ever thought possible.

"I want to fill you," he says.

I know it's supposed to be a question, and my answer should be no, but I want him to fill me too.

His hand grazes my belly. "Would your father still kill me if I were the father of your child? If this belly was swollen with our baby?"

I sit up on my elbows and stare at him because what the fuck is this baby talk and why do I like it? No, I don't want to get pregnant. Yet. But fuck if I don't love the idea of him filling and impregnating me. Would my father let us back in if he knew I was carrying a child? Somehow, I still don't know if he would.

"Vance," I say, my voice stern. Now isn't the time for this.

His hand moves toward my mouth, and he places the red tinged fingers between my parted lips before putting them in his own. "I won't do it tonight if that's not what you want, but I will fill your sweet little cunt the next time I fuck you."

He grips the base of his dick and pulls out of me. Warm, slick skin brushes my clit as he strokes himself and comes on my pussy. The heat of his pleasure drips toward my entrance, and I moan. I almost tell him to put his cock back inside me so that warmth can fill what now feels so empty.

Vance tucks himself away and zips up his slacks. He looks around, smiles, and grabs the handkerchief from Antonio's pocket. After shaking it open, he cleans me off, sending a different kind of shiver through my body.

Then he asks the question I still don't have an answer to.

"So will you be coming with me, little girl?"

CHAPTER TWENTY-SEVEN

Vance

Her eyes drop to her husband's body. If she really wanted to, she could blame me for all this and live her life in peace. I'd let her. Even though her family's soldiers would come after me, I'd sacrifice myself so she could return to her normal life if that's what she wants.

She'd probably be married off to the next schmuck her family elects to hand her off to, but this is a decision she has to make. She can choose the life she's always known, or she can choose to come with me.

It's a big ask. We'll spend our life hiding from both sides if she takes a chance on me. I can't give her the expensive cars or luxury housing she's accustomed to, either. If I were her, I'd be inclined to blame it all on me.

"Vance," she says as she sits up.

I seek the least bit of intel on what direction she's leaning, but her voice is level, her expression unreadable.

I step into her and pull her to her feet. "Tell me."

I need her to tell me because I can't wait a moment longer

for her answer. My fate rests in her soft hands. Will I run from her or with her?

"Running away with you is suicide," she whispers.

My shoulders drop.

"So I guess I'm suicidal." Her dark eyes round as the corners of her lips draw upward.

I guess we both are. And there's no one else I'd rather die beside.

I lean into her and kiss her. "I'll make you come every day until then."

She licks her lips as she pulls away from me. "Hopefully it doesn't hurt like that every time."

I reach behind my back, draw my second pistol, and offer it to her. She smiles and takes the gun, then checks to see if it's loaded with such sexy effortlessness, like she was born with a gun in her hand. Considering this family, she may have been.

Her dark eyes flash with a fire I haven't seen before. "Well, let's get this shit show on the road."

SHE GRABBED her bag on the way out. She hadn't even unpacked anything before he tried to get beneath her dress. But in his defense, I'm not sure I would have been able to wait half as long as he did. I probably would have thrown her ass against that marble wall and fucked her in front of her entire family at the ceremony. Would have spread her thighs and made her bleed in front of her own blood.

Either way, it made it much easier to abduct her from her guarded ivory tower.

We sit in the car, and excitement courses through both of

us. Her chest rises and falls with each heavy breath. Then she throws back her head and laughs.

"What the hell are we doing!" she screams.

It's not a question. We're very much aware of what we're doing. We're making a life-altering decision to be together, which could end up with one or both of us dead.

"Being incredibly stupid," I tell her as I throw the car in reverse.

She shrugs. "Or smart."

We look at each other. We know what it is. But having her by my side will be worth all the stupidity. All the running.

She sobers and brushes back her dark hair. "Well, where are we going?"

"I have a 'safe house' of sorts." I put the car in drive and head east.

"A safe house? Why?"

"I've spent most of the last two decades guarding others from really shitty people. I've made plenty of enemies over the years."

Her eyes narrow. "I don't even have a safe house."

I chuckle. "Well *that's* stupid."

It's not like a safe house in an action movie. It's a house just outside the state, and its paper trail doesn't lead back to me. I've had to use it twice. Once when I stayed with a stripper I was trying to protect from her enraged pimp, and another time when I had to keep a witness safe until their court date. Not once have I used it to protect myself.

I normally welcome people to come at me, but I won't risk others I'm tasked with defending. If I had known how I'd feel about Isabella, I might have whisked her away to my safe house to keep her from being forced into marriage in the first place, but I didn't realize just how strong my feelings were until they took her from me.

Now I plan to only be away from her if there's no more

life in my body. I will die before I let them take her away again.

I reach over and caress the back of her neck. "I'm glad you came with me."

"I didn't really have a choice. I wasn't going to sick my father's dogs on you or put the blame on you when I'm just as guilty for making you fall in love with me." A smirk tugs at her lips.

I scoff. "I-I don't . . ." My voice trails off.

I want to tell her she didn't make me fall in love with her. I've never spoken those words to a woman so candidly, and I don't know if I can say them. It's hard enough to let myself feel that way. But I can't deny the truth of her accusation. After all, you don't risk your life like this for someone you don't love.

CHAPTER TWENTY-EIGHT

Isabella

We pull up to the small house in the middle of nowhere Connecticut. Honestly, the bathroom at my house was probably as big as this whole place.

Towering trees surround us on all sides, and the smell of late-night dew wafts toward my nose as soon as I open the car door. I stand and stretch my legs, then I take a good look around at the place.

One faint yellow light illuminates the small concrete porch. Spiderwebs criss-cross and twist around the rusting white metal fixture. It's so much different from the home I came from.

Home.

It can never be my home again. I've turned my back on my flesh and blood.

It still stings a little to think of what I've left behind, even though my father sold me off like livestock. I'm more than a prized broodmare with a mile-long pedigree, though. I could have had an entire world laid out in front of me if I just stayed married to Antonio, but I'm not that kind of girl and that wasn't the life I wanted for myself. Why my father thought I'd be complacent when I've always been anything but is beyond me.

But I guess it didn't help that I went along with it, even if I knew I'd be miserable for all of eternity. So maybe I'm more of an accomplice to my own unhappiness than I want to believe.

Regardless, Vance threw a wrench into the machine my father and the Vendettis built. Any bit of expected normalcy was shattered the moment he made me come. I could no longer remain a bitch on a leash once I tasted the freedom I'd been denied for so many years.

The light flicks on in front of me, and Vance's arms wrap around my waist before he pulls me inside. "I know it's much shittier here than a princess like you deserves," he says, his mouth dropping to my shoulder.

"Shut up. It's perfect," I say.

It's old and small, and the furniture looks like it's seen better days. The appliances appear to be older than I am—maybe even older than my father. Paint flakes at the seam where the ceiling meets the wall. But Vance is here, and *that* makes it perfect. I'd walk into a cardboard box with a smile on my face if it was Vance's fucking box.

"Do you think they found Antonio yet?" I ask.

"They probably found him as soon as they found out what I did to their guards." His expression shifts into sadistic plea-sure, as if he thoroughly enjoyed what he's done. What he did for me. And what he's done goes right to the juncture between my legs too.

As if sensing the growing heat between my thighs, he spins me around and pushes me against the wall. His lips find mine, heavy and hungry.

I pull away to take a breath. "Have you ever had sex with anyone here?"

His eyebrow lifts. "The women I've had here were clients. Nothing more. You know I take my job very seriously."

"Serious as murder," I say with a smirk. "Does that mean I get to be a first for you?"

He laughs. "You've been plenty of firsts for me, Bella. I've never driven as a woman dry-humped my leg. I've never fucked a virgin. Or a mafia princess. Oh yeah, or committed multiple homicides and abducted said princess."

I smirk. "Guess we're even."

"Nowhere near," he growls. His hands clamp around my waist before he lifts me and sets me on top of the worn countertop in the kitchen.

My hands drop between my legs. "No way. I need to shower," I tell him. We drove for hours after he fucked me. A shower is for sure in my very near future.

He wipes my hair from my face. "I don't care how dirty you feel. I'm just going to make you dirtier."

I nearly choke on his words. My mouth just stutters. But still, no.

"Hard pass." I push him away from me and drop to the floor. "Which way to the bathroom, daddy?"

He growls and grabs my hand, dragging me toward the room down the hall. Before I can even close the door, he's ripped my dress from my body and stripped himself as well. Shadows bloom beneath every hard curve of muscle, and I can't take my eyes away. He's mouthwatering.

And he's mine.

He turns on the water and stares at me, his hand wrapped around his chin in the most delicious look of restraint. I get in the shower, the cool water pebbling my skin. A quick turn of the old knob brings needed warmth to my body. The warmth only grows when Vance steps inside, sandwiches me against the wall, and closes the door behind him.

He grabs a bottle of body wash and pours it into his open hand, then he runs it over my naked body. The soap builds to a slippery lather on my skin, and his slick fingers glide over my abdomen and down my hips. His hands move to my ass, rubbing and squeezing as he cleans me.

I've never been washed like that. It's an out-of-body experience, as if I'm floating above us as his powerful touch rubs away every ounce of dirt, tension, and pain. His hands move to my breasts, and he holds their weight before letting them slip through his grasp. His palms brush my nipples, but his touch doesn't linger. He continues to cleanse and tease me.

A moan leaves my lips. "Daddy," I whisper.

His soapy hand floats between my legs, cleaning away the dried blood and come. "So clean," he growls. "I can't wait to make you filthy again."

He plucks the showerhead from the caddy and rinses me off. My head drops back, and I breathe in the clean scent. My hair becomes a silk curtain draping down my back. His fingers work through the strands until he entangles himself and pulls me to my knees.

His cock stands erect in front of my face. Using my hair as a handlebar, he pushes my lips onto him and impales the back of my throat. The way he moves me is so hungry. Driven. Like I belong to him. I guess I kind of do.

Vance's hand rests beneath my chin and slides back toward my throat as he fucks it. He feels so much bigger in my mouth, stretching my throat.

"Good fucking girl," he growls.

A warm, floating feeling washes over me as his fingers squeeze one side of my neck and his thumb constricts the other. My eyes roll to the back of my head.

"Play with your pussy," he whispers. "I want to feel your orgasm through your throat."

I do as he tells me, with the warm floating feeling still carrying me, and drop my hand between my legs. I stroke myself in tight circles. My fingers swirl in bigger loops as my hips buck against the pleasure. He fucks my face, and it makes me throb. Cool water drips down my back and adds another layer of sensations.

"You're tightening around me. Your teeth are raking my skin as you get close. Come for me so I can spill my load down your throat."

I dig the fingers of my free hand into his thigh as the pleasure brews between mine. An intense cyclone of feelings swirls between my legs. The powerful, mind-bending force heats my skin from my pelvis to my face.

Tears stream down my cheeks as I come, as his cock drives deeper and makes me gag. The warm flood of liquid between my legs matches what slips down my throat, and I gag again as he pulls his cock from my mouth.

The taste is terrible. The texture? Even worse. But it's Vance, and I'll take anything he gives me.

I'll take it all. Even a life so different from what I'm used to.

CHAPTER TWENTY-NINE

Vance

The clock hums on the nightstand beside me. It's a sound that grows louder, despite never changing tone in reality. I reach back and tug the old rubber cord from the wall. It silences the hum, but somehow the silence is worse.

I'm on edge. Deservedly so. All I could think about was getting to Isabella. Taking out whoever I had to in order to get my hands on her again. And I did just that.

But at what cost? At what risk?

For a moment, I wonder if it's all worth it, but as I replay our time together, I realize that it absolutely is.

Soft snores permeate the silence. Isabella's asleep beside me. Sound a-fucking-sleep. I don't know how she's sleeping like a rocked baby after the murders and running away. Maybe that's just another difference between us. I may be a killer for hire, but she's been born and bred around death and destruction.

But it doesn't matter. I worried for a second if she'd

adjust. If we made the right choice. But she sure looks content as shit. So I'd say so.

"Little girl," I whisper as I turn onto my side and pull her into me.

She whimpers.

My hand slides around her and between her bare legs. "Will you wake up for me? So I can pour this frustration into you."

"Yes, *daddy?*" she says with a snark in her tired voice.

Her legs spread for me. I lift her thigh and put it over my own. With my other hand, I tug down the front of my boxers. My cock rests against her slick, wet slit. Her back arches, stroking herself against my length. I groan. She's so tempting. Delicious.

I grab her hip firmly in one hand and my cock in the other, then give her exactly what she wants. My cock impales her wet and welcoming cunt. She envelops me, nearly to my balls. She's so fucking warm. She's hugging my cock with her clenching walls.

"Fuck," she whimpers.

I pull her into me to try to give her that final bit of my length, but she can't take any more of me. I know she would if she could, but I've reached the end of her. I can tell not only by how she feels but how the tone of her moan changes. Like there's pain stringing alongside the pleasure.

I hook my arm around her and grab her chest from beneath her cami. Her breast fills my hand. I squeeze, changing those moans once again. God, she's addictive, and it's hard to believe she's mine. I feel so blessed to be graced by her very presence, let alone have it around my dick.

I release her breast and bring my hand to her throat. I use my fingers around her chin to turn her face toward me. My forehead touches hers, and it feels so fucking good. Her moans against my mouth. The sweat on her skin from the pleasure I'm giving her.

"I . . ." I begin, but I can't finish my sentence. I've never felt so strongly for another human being in my life. As if my heart and soul fully belonged to her. So why can't I tell her that? Why does it hang up in my throat when I feel it the most. Fucking A.

Before she can question my silence, I drop my hand between her legs and rub her again. Stroking her clit in feather strokes before increasing the intensity as if strumming an instrument. Her mouth calls out each stroke to the tune of my fingertips.

"I'm going to come," she says. Her walls tighten around me.

"I know, Bella. Come for me," I growl.

Her spasms wrench my dick. Fuck. She feels amazing. I want to come, so fucking bad. Fill her pussy. Fuck, fill her womb for all I care. I just need to come inside her.

"Let me fill you."

"Vance," she moans, but I hear the hesitation in my name. "You shouldn't."

"Of course I shouldn't. But I want to. Need to. No matter what happens, you're mine, Isabella. If you get knocked up. If you don't. I'm not going anywhere. You aren't going anywhere. I'll always take care of you." My voice strains as I thrust, deep, slow, and try to keep from coming. "Take me, all of me."

"Yes, daddy," she strangles out. It's not snarky. It's full of lust. Longing. I fucking love it. The word draws the come from the depths of my balls. I fill her tight little pussy. *My* tight little pussy.

With my cock still engulfed in her warmth, I hear a creak outside the door. I throw a hand over her mouth, silencing everything aside from that ominous sound.

I draw my hips back and pull out of her. I release her mouth as I reach for my gun on the nightstand and pull up my boxers. "If it comes down to me and you, choose you."

"No," she says. Not unexpectedly either. She reaches over and grabs the gun I gave her back at her shitty husband's house. "I'm not losing you again."

I grip her chin. "We knew this was coming. I just didn't think it would be so soon. I don't have nearly as many dogs in the fight as I'd like to have. If they want to take you back, and if I'm a goner, you know what you have to do."

"I won't," she says, ripping her chin from my grasp. "We either both get out or neither of us do."

"You'd die for me, Isabella?"

"Like you'd kill for *me*."

I wipe a hand through my dark hair. "Let's kill or be killed then."

CHAPTER THIRTY

Isabella

Vance tosses his shirt to me, and I slip it on. I feel around for my panties, but I can't find them. Fuck. Guess I'm facing my newfound enemy without wearing any underwear.

I rack the pistol and hold it at my side. My chin rises in defiance. I don't want to be without Vance again, even if it means killing someone in my family. Or killing my own father.

I made the choice to run off with him, and it's one of the few decisions I've made on my own. I won't give that decision back to anyone else, including the man who raised me.

Footsteps plod from somewhere in the house. An ominous thunder rings out with every step. A bead of sweat drops down the back of my neck and buries itself in the shirt. Vance puts me behind him as he walks along the wall and inches toward the door. He's shirtless, wearing nothing more than his boxers, and he looks deliciously terrifying.

Vance stops and turns toward me before he reaches the

door. His hot palm caresses my cheek. Instead of comforting me, it sends a bolt of panic up my spine because it feels like goodbye.

"I love you, Isabella. If something happens to me, just know that I would do anything for you, including dying. I'd lay my life down in front of you so you can step over this steaming pile of shit we're in without getting it on your feet." He swallows. "And I'm sorry I couldn't say it sooner."

I set my jaw, refusing to accept his words like this. "Don't say it because you're certain we won't make it out of this together."

"I just need you to know." He pulls me into him and gives me a hard kiss on the mouth. It's like nothing I've ever felt. Is this what the kiss of death feels like? A final type of passion that can't be mimicked or recreated without the near certainty of death?

But this kiss isn't goodbye. I won't accept that.

"I love you, Vance, but say it to me after tonight. When you aren't facing the prospect of dying, please." I let a tight smile cross my face. It's meant to be comforting, but I've never been very good at that.

I put my hand on his chest and urge him forward. A low sigh leaves his lips before he turns toward the door, grips the handle, and rips it open.

I follow him down the dark hallway. Emptiness welcomes us on our path and pulls us toward the footsteps, which stop as soon as the sound of ours joins them. Whoever waits in the darkness knows we're here now. Now it's just a matter of coming face to face—the ominous moment when eyes meet eyes, barrels meet barrels, and everyone knows the intentions of the other.

A man grabs Vance, and they begin a battle of strength right in the small home's living room. I step forward and raise the pistol to help him, but another set of large hands wrap around my waist and pull me into a hard chest.

A familiar chest.

The scent of cigar smoke wraps around me like the arms pinning me in place, and I can no longer breathe.

My father.

His hand snakes around my wrist and wrenches the pistol from my grasp. "Isabella, I'm so disappointed in you," he says, squeezing harder.

At the sound of my whimper, Vance grinds out a primordial shout. "You better not hurt her, old man!"

With furrowed brows, my father's attention moves toward the ensuing struggle. If he only brought one soldier to deal with Vance, he should be more nervous than this.

"Let me go," I say as I struggle against my father's grip.

Grunts and groans rise from the living room floor as Vance and his assailant roll around in a heap of flailing arms and legs. A gunshot punctuates the sounds pouring from the fray, and my breath catches. I have no way of knowing who fired the gun or who's been shot. Darkness shrouds the melee. It could be either one of them. It could be both of them. The not knowing is enough to drive me insane.

My heart sinks deep into my belly, and I'd shit it out right now if I could. What would I do if I lost him? How could I live if that *I love you* was the last one before his death?

"Vance!" I yell.

My father throws a hand over my mouth and backs me toward the door. He's confident Vance is the injured party and sees no way his soldier would lose. It's incomprehensible to him, but the alternative is incomprehensible to *me*.

He drags me further toward the door, and I kick and fight with everything in me. He whips open the door, and cool night air hits me as he pulls me toward the car. His hand releases my mouth, and my screams immediately follow.

"You sold me off to a monster!" I shout.

"You were supposed to do two jobs as my only daughter. Get married. Create an empire."

"Fuck your empire!" I send my elbow backward, and it collides with his side.

With a breathless grunt, he releases me for a second, and I make a run for it. His fingers wrap around my arm and haul me backward before I can put more than a few feet between us. Something sharp pierces the sensitive skin of my neck, and a burning sensation sends flaming fingers across my nerve endings.

My father pants, his chest heaving as he tries to support my relaxing muscles. My eyelids attempt to close, but I keep them open by sheer determination. My limbs feel disconnected from me. I lean back into my father's broad chest to keep from toppling over as the ground seems to heel like a sailboat beneath my feet.

"What did you do to me?" I ask, my words slurring.

"It's something to protect myself from you. You turned on us. Deserted your family. Chose a piece of shit like him over us."

Each heavy breath takes more effort than the last, but I draw enough air to ask the question rushing up my throat. "Are you going to kill me?"

A creepy, low laugh shakes his chest against my back. "No, Isabella." His fingers brush my hair away from my face. "It's not my place to take your life. You didn't kill *my* son."

"You're giving me to the Vendettis? Your own daughter?" Each word takes such effort, but I've never been one to shut my mouth, no matter the circumstances.

My father squeezes my throat. "You were dead to me once you severed our deal and ran off the way you did." Instead of releasing his grip, he tightens his hold around me. Black shadows cloud the corners of my vision, but I can only think of one thing as everything begins to blur.

"*Vance*," I whisper.

"He can't save you," my father hisses.

As if the fibrous connection between my brain and body has been severed, my consciousness starts to fade. My eyes close and stay that way, too heavy to open again. I can no longer hear the wind piercing the forest canopy. I can no longer smell the scent of my fear mixed with earth and moss. My brain focuses on oxygenating my most vital organs and abandons my senses entirely.

I'm sliding into a black abyss.

His grip loosens, and I'm moving away from him. I force my eyes open but see nothing in front of me. Powerful arms turn me and press me against a broad, muscled chest.

Blinking away the haze, my gaze lands on my father as he wobbles on his feet and presses his hand to his neck. He falls back against the car, and his wide eyes burn through me.

I turn my head and look up at my savior. I knew who it was as soon as my body was safely tucked against him, but I couldn't believe it until I saw him with my own eyes. Blood drips from a long gash on his face, but he's alive. And he saved me.

"Vance," I whisper. My eyes fall to his hand. An empty syringe pokes from his fist. My father's soldier must have had one for Vance, but it's clear who got to it first. "Are you going to kill him too?" I ask as I peer into his face.

I hate to admit it, but I don't wish death upon my father. I just want him to leave me alone. If he thinks I'm dead to him, let me be dead.

Vance holds me closer, surrounding me in his warmth and safety as he looks into my eyes and says, "I have some words for your father before I decide."

CHAPTER THIRTY-ONE

Vance

Her father is still fast asleep. And very much tied to a chair in the living room. My hand brushes through Isabella's hair. He underestimated me, and he knows better. Or have I underestimated him? He only brought one soldier, but more could arrive if he doesn't report in soon.

As if reading my mind, Isabella steps away from me, goes to her father, and fishes through his pocket. She lifts his phone and uses his sleeping face to open it. Her fingers move in a flurry as she sends a text and sets the phone on the table beside him.

"What'd you do?" I ask.

She smirks. "I told them it's done. If we didn't, they'd send more men."

I may not be a part of their life, but we're on the same page there. The last thing we want is for the cavalry to come for her next.

My hand wraps up in her hair, and I drag her into me. "So fucking smart," I growl.

She leans into me and I capture her mouth, completely ignoring the fact that her father sleeps just feet away as my tongue dances with hers. When I step into her until her back hits the wall, she whimpers.

"What if I wanted to fuck you in front of your father?" I ask.

A warm breath leaves her lips. "I can't," she pants.

My eyebrow rises. "I didn't expect Isabella Angotti to be shy." My hand moves up her bare thighs, raising the hem of the oversized t-shirt she's wearing.

"I'm not shy!"

"Then suck my dick in front of your father," I whisper.

Her hands wash down my body as she drops to her knees. She tugs down my boxers, and my cock springs to life in front of her face. I'm constantly hard around this girl.

Bella's mouth wraps around me, and I thrust my hips to meet her movements. My hand grips the back of her head and encourages her. I drop back my head and release a groan from the depths of my belly because her mouth feels like fucking heaven.

"Goddamn it, Isabella, you feel so good."

I look over and see her father stirring. I'm tempted to stop her, but he'll be drowsy for a little longer. I fuck her throat harder and faster. I love that he might witness my cock in his sweet little girl's mouth. Fucking her face.

He murmurs something, and my balls tighten until the pleasure bearing down on me grows intolerable.

"I'm going to come," I growl. "Daddy's going to come right in front of your father."

"Please," she begs. Her lips spread for me, and I jerk my cock in front of her face to spill the pearls of pleasure onto her beautiful tongue. Her father's groan echoes mine as I finish on his beloved daughter.

On my beloved Bella.

My girl.

"I love you so fucking much, and I'm not saying that because of an imminent risk of death. I'm saying it with my come on your tongue because I want you to swallow those feelings I have for you. I want to be a part of what's inside you."

Isabella licks the come off her lips like the boss bitch she is and smiles up at me. "Love you too, daddy," she says with a playful waggle of her tongue.

Speaking of daddies, we need to deal with her actual father. His glassy eyes focus on me as I put away my cock.

"Morning, father of the year," I say as I drag his head back by his hair.

"You sick fuck," he hisses, a tired, dazed ebb in his tone.

"I'm sick because I played with your daughter consensually, but you're A-OK with the fact that her 'husband' tried to force himself on her? Makes sense." I inhale. "Or are you mad that your daughter wants to be with *me*, but not the man you picked for her?"

"You don't understand this life, Lore, and I don't expect you to understand, but you have no idea what you've done."

"What do I have to do to get you to accept us and our desire to be together? I don't need you to like it, but I need you to leave us the fuck alone."

"I won't ever accept it," he says.

I pull a knife from my pocket and press the blade to his throat. "Then I'll have to kill you."

"You wouldn't."

I would. I really fucking would. But we can't run from them forever.

I rip the knife from his throat and go for his dick. All men value that over their lives.

"Wait!" he yells, a mere centimeter from me giving him a bloody new piercing. "Let's talk, you fucking psychopath."

"I'm not a psychopath. You and your people just don't like anyone willing to challenge you." I gesture toward Isabella. "For her, I'll challenge any one of you. All of you."

"What about your affair?" Isabella's sing-song voice comes up behind me.

"My what?" her father asks.

"I know you're fucking that twenty-something-year-old you hired," she says. "I saw it."

"What the fuck does that matter?"

She smirks. "If my mother's family found out, it wouldn't go over well for you. You'd lose anything you didn't create yourself. And that's quite a lot, isn't it, father? Grandpa's investments got you to where you are today."

Angelino's eyes narrow. "Are you kidding me, Isabella? Blackmailing your own father?"

Isabella laughs. "Let's not play who has more morals here."

He exhales, low and slow. "What do you want to keep your mouth shut?"

"To be left alone." She looks at me. "With Vance."

"Then you will have absolutely nothing from me. You know that, right? Nothing."

She scoffs. "I want nothing from you, aside from turning a blind eye."

While they talk, I walk into my kitchen and draw up a quick contract. It states that Isabella is mine, that they are to fuck right off about us, and that he, as the head of his family, gives us his blessing to exit the life.

I return to the living room and throw the contract into his face. "Sign this. It says that you'll leave us alone. For good."

His dark eyes narrow on me. "I need my fucking hand for that."

I release one hand and throw the pen into his lap. Once he's scrawled his signature on the line, I whip his hand upward, take the knife, and cut his palm. "Sign it with blood, too. We know how important that is to your families."

That's an oath he can't go back on, though we all know how much integrity the man has. But I'll be ready if he goes back on it. I will *always* be ready.

"You sure about this?" I ask Isabella, before we both sign.

"I've never been more certain about anything, Vance," she says with a confident nod.

Isabella is willing to throw away everything she knew about her old life to build a life with me that will never offer the luxury and grandeur she was used to. I can offer her different things, though. I just hope I can make her happy.

And I hope she's making the right choice, because there's no coming back from this.

With all three signatures on the paper, a satisfied smile slides onto her face. She turns to me and raises her eyebrows. "Now kill him."

CHAPTER THIRTY-TWO

Isabella

"Are you sure?" Vance asks, his eyebrow rising. My father flails and panics, and Vance struggles to keep him pinned against the chair. "You don't think he'll keep his promise?"

I shake my head. "I know he won't. Because I wouldn't."

Vance smirks. "Are any of you guys honest?"

A smirk tugs at my own lips. "When we want to be. But he'd never leave us alone. We'd never be able to stay together if he's allowed to leave here."

"Yes, I would leave you alone!" My father's words filter through a throat strained with panic. "You will *never* see me again. I swear to God!"

"Like we swore to God that I was entering a marriage I wanted?"

"God damn it, Isabella. Don't be stupid. You can't kill me without causing an earthquake within this family. You'll destroy everything!"

I roll my eyes. "That's the point. If the family is in ruins, they can't come after us. None of you can come after us."

"You stupid, stupid girl," he hisses.

Vance draws back his arm and punches my father in the face. Blood pours from his nose. "Be respectful or shut the fuck up, old man."

A fine spray of blood spews from his mouth as he spits. He turns to me. "So you'll kill me, get some of my life insurance money, and run off into the wind with your little *bodyguard?* Is that your little plan?"

I wrap my hand around my chin. "I hadn't thought about life insurance. Thanks, Dad." I turn to Vance. "Do it."

He looks at me as if he thinks I should turn away before he acts, as if what I might witness will be too much for my mind to bear. He doesn't yet grasp that my allegiance lies with him.

My eyes harden on my father, and I hand the knife to Vance. He doesn't bother asking for reassurance again. The confidence I feel about my decision must be written all over my face.

"Isabella, no!" my father pleads, trying to get to the last shred of human decency inside me.

Plot twist: there isn't one.

When my expression doesn't change, he tries to plead with the man he hired. "Vance, I've given you work when you had nothing. Don't let her take advantage of you. Isabella is using you. She's a black widow. You'll be next."

A black widow? I was a widow in a white dress.

My gaze leaps to Vance, and I try to read his expression. Does he believe my father's lies? Is it enough to make him doubt everything we have? His heavy brows pull together, uncertainty dancing in his eyes, but then he draws back his arm and repeatedly sends a fist into my father's face until he can't talk any more shit.

Vance won't be swayed. Thank fuck.

My eyes flame as he tightens his grip on the knife and drives the blade into my father's gut. With a grunt, he twists and pushes it deeper. I grew up with the sounds of murder. It's like a lullaby. Secretly, I live for it. And I hate that because it means I have become what Vance thinks I am. A monster among monsters.

By the time the lullaby ends, my father's breaths are mere gurgles.

"Daddy," I whisper as tears fill my eyes.

"I'm sorry, Isabella," Vance apologizes. He must think he sees regret in my eyes.

I step toward the two men, and my fingers graze the blood on my father's face before I turn to Vance. "Not him. You."

His lips draw into a smirk. He drops the knife and wraps his powerful arms around me. "My little girl."

"Fuck me," I say, shooting a quick glance toward my father's dead body.

"Now? In front of—"

"Yes, Vance. You got yours, and now I'd like to get mine."

"You are so sick and twisted, Isabella," he growls.

"More twisted than having me suck your cock in front of him when he was alive?"

Vance smirks. "Fair."

I step back until my spine hits the wall, then I raise the hem of my shirt. The slow shake of his head stops, turning into a subtle nod with a lick of his lips. I knew he'd give in to me. He'll do anything for me. And I'll do anything for him.

Vance walks into me, and his hard cock battles the few morals he has. The angel on his shoulder tells him Daddy shouldn't fuck me and fill me in front of my dead father. But the devil on his shoulder—me—demands it.

"I need you inside me," I whisper, dragging my bloody

fingers up my thighs, leaving a trail of red on my skin. His eyes hyper-fixate on the crimson. A feral growl leaves his throat.

"I'd do anything for you," he says. "Fall for you. Kill for you."

"Then give me your cock," I whisper.

Vance looks back at my father's body before stepping into me and rubbing his palms up my legs. He pulls down his boxers, lifts my thigh, and presses the head of his massive cock to my entrance. He pushes inside me. There's no resistance because I'm still so wet from sucking his cock.

His hand wraps around the front of my throat as he impales me with his cock, driving his hips into me. He fucks my family bloodline out of me. Fucks my family name from me. And I want him to replace my last name with his.

"Marry me, Vance," I scream through a moan.

He stops thrusting. His hand loosens its grip on my throat. That devilishly handsome face twists into something unfamiliar, and I'm not sure what it means.

I didn't mean to yell my thoughts. In the heat of the moment, as he rearranged my guts, it just came out. In hindsight, it was such a stupid thing to say. I wish I could take it back. Fuck, the last thing I want is to look like an idiot. To be rejected by—

"Any-fucking-time, little girl," he says before kissing me hard enough to silence my panicked thoughts.

"Really?" My voice is a breathless whisper when he pulls away.

"I'd happily be another victim of the black widow," he says through a smirk.

I bite his neck with a laugh. "If I was going to be a predatory insect, I'd be a praying mantis. You'd have to make me come before I killed you."

Vance gives me a forceful thrust that strangles a moan

from me. "God, I love you. And look, I'm saying it balls deep in your pussy with your father's blood on my hands. Do you believe me yet?"

My cheeks flush. "I think I do."

Vance fucks me harder. Faster. Until I'm a trembling mess in front of him. The pressure brews between my legs as I approach the edge.

"You're tightening on me, Bella. Come for me and tell me you love me as you spasm around my dick."

His dark, gravelly words go right to my vagina. I scoop my hips as the vibrations rumble through my core. I seize on his cock, coming until I'm nearly blind. I've never known such an intense, breath-stealing orgasm.

"I fucking love you, Vance." The words strangle from me as I scream out.

"Good fucking girl." He holds me, keeping me from collapsing as the trembles quiver through every muscle in my body. He leans closer and presses his mouth to my ear. "Now . . . do you plan to kill me, or will you let me live?"

I study his eyes, his handsome face, and I can only come to one conclusion. "I think I'll keep you around."

EPILOGUE

Vance

There's no family here for us on our "big day." Just a simple wedding that I feel is less than she deserves. Most people like her expect extravagant settings and would settle for nothing less, but here she is, a big smile on her face at the tiny local courthouse in front of a judge.

"You've been married before?" the woman at the desk turns to Isabella and asks.

I lean against the counter and put my fist in front of my mouth to keep from exposing my smirk. She was married for a few hours before I made her a widow.

The clerk is just trying to make conversation, but it's unnecessary. We already answered these questions when we applied for the license.

"Oh yes, I'm a widow," Isabella announces, the sullen tone in her voice clearly rehearsed.

"That's so sad," the secretary says.

Isabella kicks me beneath the desk. "Absolutely tragic."

The woman's lips tighten before she forces a smile. "Well,

let's make this a happier day, then. You two are getting married! Love finds a way!"

Her overenthusiasm needs to be toned the fuck down. When I was buried in Isabella's pussy, I promised her I'd marry her, and I intend to do exactly that. But we already feel married. How can we not, after what we've been through? We're bound by blood at this point.

We're ushered into the courthouse—me in my suit, Isabella in a stunning purple dress, and the judge and a court witness. The ceremony breezes by as it's intended to. Trans-actional. I just need Isabella to be my wife.

Mine.

"I now pronounce you husband and wife," the judge says. Silver frames perch on his aging face. "You may kiss the bride."

I pull Isabella into me and kiss her so deeply that it has to be a sin to do this in front of a judge. But I can't help it. She's mine. Physically, mentally, and now on paper. Officially.

My hand laces through her dark hair, and I draw her closer to my body. Her heat warms me. She whimpers, and each breath between us is owned by us both.

"My car. Now," I whisper in her ear. "We'll be right back. We forgot something in the car," I say to the staff.

Her shitty ex-husband waited so much longer than I ever could to get my hands on my new bride. I can't even leave the fucking building without thinking about being inside her. We hardly make it to the SUV before I'm on her. I pull her into the backseat and slam the door. She straddles my lap and I kiss her.

"Daddy," she whispers as she grinds her hips on my lap. Even with a perfectly good dick to ride, she still loves the feeling of my slacks and zipper against her pussy. Who am I to stop her as she rides me and chases her pleasure?

"Right now, Bella, you're going to call me your husband." I need to hear that word.

She increases the tempo with her hips, grinding her wet fucking pussy along the front of my pants. She's going to make me walk into that courthouse to sign the paperwork with a trail of her come on my slacks. And I'll wear it proudly.

Her fingers grip the shoulders of my dress shirt. She bends her neck and buries her face into my chest with a melodic moan. I always know when she's close. Even without being inside her. Even as she just rocks her hips on my lap.

"Come for me, wife," I growl. I get almost nothing from her dry-humping me—an ache as she brushes my cock with her gyrations—but fuck if it doesn't mentally make me bust when she comes by using my body for her sole pleasure.

She screams out as she orgasms. Her voice is hoarse and sultry at the tail end of her moan. "I love you, husband," she says.

I reach between us, draw my zipper down, and pull out my cock so I can fuck her through her pulsing orgasm. Fill the vacant space. I push inside her, so warm and wet for me. I don't even recognize the tone of my groan, so rabid with need. Her spasming pussy pulses around me. It's like sinking into a vise, and I'm not even complaining. She's just so perfect.

"I love you, Bella," I whisper as I grip her hair and crane her neck for a kiss.

Spilling my load inside her hasn't knocked her up yet. Maybe there is a God, and maybe he knows I don't deserve children, but fuck if it doesn't keep me from trying to fuck, fill, and breed her. Put a smudge of a person inside her high-class womb. A bodyguard's spawn inside a mafia queen.

I put my hand on her lower belly as I grab her hip and pull her against my lap to fill her again. Knowing that my wife's pussy is now spasming around me only guaranteed I wouldn't last long.

"Will you always protect me, daddy?" she whispers, a pleasure-filled exhale drifting between us.

"Until my final breath, little girl."

We peel away from each other and I put my come-soaked cock away. She lowers her dress as if I didn't just consummate the marriage before we even finished signing the fucking license.

We walk back into the courthouse and the judge and witness stop what they're doing and stare at us. We look like we didn't forget anything at all. Like we went to the car to just fuck. Which is precisely what we did.

The witness' eyes stop on the front of my pants, right on the very distinguishable wet spot. I pull Isabella in front of me to obscure the sight. Her cheeks flush red, but I accept the accusatory glares proudly.

Yeah, I fucked my beautiful wife outside of a courthouse. It's not the worst thing I've done for her.

And now that we have our entire lives ahead of us, I'll do whatever it takes to keep my little girl safe, no matter who or what tries to stand in our way. I've spent my entire career protecting what belongs to others. Now I finally get to protect what's mine. My wife.

This ebook originated as a serial romance on Patreon, where Lauren's reader-driven stories are shared weekly. Join to be a part of Spicy Story Sundays! www.patreon.com/ LaurenBielAuthor

Check out my ride or die hitchhiker romances

Books2read.com/Hitched
Books2read.com/Mfmhitchhiker
Books2read.com/DrivingMyObsession
Books2read.com/AcrossStateLines
For more novellas:
Books2read.com/HerFantasy
Books2read.com/StrangerSession
Books2read.com/Wantednovella
Books2read.com/Dont-Stop

CONNECT WITH LAUREN

Don't miss a thing from Lauren Biel! Check out all of her books, social media connections, and other important information at Campsite.bio/LaurenBielAuthor and LaurenBiel.com

ACKNOWLEDGMENTS

To my VIP gals (Lori, Kimberly, Jessie, Nikita, Lexi, Grace), I love you so much!

Thank you to my husband for being MY protector!

Thank you to my editor for dealing with me!

Thank you to my valued Patrons. Your contribution helped make this book happen!

Lori R, Jessie, Michelle M, Tabitha F, Lindsey S, Erika M, Laura T, Nicole M, Nineette W, Kimberly B, BoneDaddy-Ashe, Kimberly S, Sammi Rae, Sarah, Allison B, Andrea J, Chelle, Gabby S, Jennifer H, Jessica G, Samantha R, Sara S,@bethbetweenthepages, Sharee S, Samantha W, Lourdes G, Kelli T, Shelby F, Lauren P, Mackenzie H, Tiannah B, Wombles, Kristiana B, Vero A, Deani, Amanda C, Brooke O, Liza M, Ashley P, Mandy, Maddy, Courtney P, Kate, Lisa A, Leslie W, Mrs Mandy, Jordyn J, DJ Krimmer, Kayla M, Marisa, Jess M, Amber, Tiffany T, Smitty, Anna S, Barrie, Ruth, Alexandria R, Brianne, Leeat, DirtyPanda, Callie K, Christine Powell, Erica W, Ashley T

ALSO BY LAUREN BIEL

To view Lauren Biel's complete list of books, visit: https://laurenbiel.com/laurenbielbooks/

ABOUT THE AUTHOR

Lauren Biel is the author of many dark romance books, with several more titles in the works. When she's not working, she's writing. When she's not writing, she's spending time with her husband, her friends, or her pets. You might also find her on a horseback trail ride or sitting beside a waterfall in Upstate New York. When reading her work, expect the unexpected. To be the first to know about her upcoming titles, please visit www.LaurenBiel.com.